The Case of the Courtlandt Jewels

By G. H. Teed

First Published in the Sexton Blake Library, No. 253.
Series 1, 31 Oct. 1922.

Cover by Arthur Jones

A Dr. Huxton Rymer Detective Adventure Romance.

Stillwoods Edition 2019.

Stillwoods.Blogspot.Ca

5 NOVEMBER NUMBERS 5

OF THE

 **SEXTON BLAKE LIBRARY**

No. 253

The Riders of the Sands.

A wonderful tale of Sexton Blake and Tinker, introducing Granite Grant (the King's Spy) and Mademoiselle Julie.

No. 259

The Case of the Woman in Black.

A story of baffling mystery and clever deduction, By the author of "The Case of the Paralysed Man," etc.

No. 260

The Lighthouse Mystery;

or, The Pirates of Hango.

A fascinating tale of thrilling adventure, featuring Dr. Ferraro. By the author of "By the Skin of his Teeth," etc.

No. 261

The Earl's Return.

A magnificent detective-adventure story with an amazing plot. Specially written by the author of "The Taming of Neville Ibbetson," etc., etc.

No. 262

The Rajah of Ghanapore.

A splendid detective romance of India, introducing Sexton Blake v. Gunga Dass.

 **Please order your copies early.**
Do not wait until next month.

ii

Catalogue Information

Title: The Case of the Courtlandt Jewels
Author: G. H. Teed (1886-1938)
Originally published in the Sexton Blake Library, No. 253. Series 1, 31 Oct. 1922.
Cover originally illustrated by Arthur Jones and adapted.
This Edition: Stillwoods, 2019
ISBN Canada: 978-1-988304-80-9
Blog: Stillwoods.Blogspot.Ca
Author's Blog: http://ghteed.blogspot.com/
Storefront: http://www.lulu.com/spotlight/lulubook22

Keywords: Sexton Blake, The Black Eagle, British detective fiction

Synopsis

Dr. Huxton Rymer, an antagonist of detective Sexton Blake, has settled down to a seemingly honest life in rural England. But the temptations of crime are a bit to attractive to him and one proposal is just too tantalizing and inventive to be resisted.

The results of that crime literally drop from the sky to Tinker's amazement—but the resolution takes Blake even to Paris where Rymer introduces the lovely and capable Mary Trent.

This is the first story that includes her.

The advertisements appeared in the original magazine. /drf

Printed and Published on the first Friday in each month by the Proprietors, The Amalgamated
Press (1922), Ltd., The Fleetway House, Farringdon St., London E.C.4. Advertisement Offices:
The Fleetway House, Farringdon Street, London, E.C.4. Subscription Rates: Single Copies,
Inland, 5d.; Abroad, 4½d. each. Registered for transmission by Canadian Magazine Post. Sole
Agents for South Africa: The Central News Agency, Limited. Sole Agents for Australia and
New Zealand: Messrs. Gordon & Gotch, Limited; and for Canada, the Imperial News Co., Limited.

iv

CHAPTER 1.   The New Tenant of Abbey Towers—Rymer's Elaborate Scheme—A Chance Meeting with Sexton Blake—A Visitor Who Was Seeking for Advice.

DR. HUXTON RYMER, known in certain highly intellectual and exclusive social circles as Professor Andrew Butterfield, and in other strata of society as the "Doc.," lighted a choice Havana and expelled a cloud of blue smoke across the white cloth of his dining-table with slow satisfaction.

His gaze wandered about the room, taking in contentedly the rich furnishings and selected paintings which made it so agreeable to his sense of the aesthetic.

It was the sort of room he had dreamed of for years as possessing; the sort of room which he had dreamed of for years as being but one apartment of many—would be but one unit in that whole which would go to make up a small, but desirable country estate. And at last his dreams had come true.

Abbey Towers had come into the market at exactly the right time for Rymer. It was a small country estate of a little over a hundred acres, in one of the most beautiful parts of Sussex, a few miles out of Horsham. It lay on the slope of a gentle rise, facing the distant downs—a well-wooded piece of land, with a small stream bounding it on two sides, wooded country on a third side, and the road on the fourth.

The house itself—originally an old English abbey, whose twin sentinel towers had given the place its name—had been built well back from the road, and was hidden from passing traffic by the old trees which were dotted about the miniature park. That was on the east.

On the south and west the ground sloped down through a thick tangle of trees and shrubs to the stream, with a maze of attractive paths intersecting in every direction. On the north, the ground rose slightly to the wood which adjoined the estate, and which was used by Rymer's neighbour only in the shooting season.

The house itself had received many alterations and additions by various owners during the past few hundred years, but some freak of luck had preserved its fine, original lines from the insult of the incongruous. The main front, with the two towers at either end, was almost as it had been built by the monks of old.

A third storey had been added in Elizabethan times by one tenant, but had so been incorporated with the existing pile as not to dwarf the towers. Wings had then been thrown out on the north and south sides, and, later on, in Georgian times, the back had been extended.

The tenant of the early Victorian period had contented himself with repairs and very slight alterations, although a small, but fine block of stables had been built on the north side about a hundred yards from the house. Then this tenant's grandson (whose death had brought the place into the market) had brought it up to date in Edwardian years by the installation of the most modern forms of lighting, heating, and sanitation, leaving the new owner little to make in the form of expenditure beyond what his fancy might dictate.

It had been described by the agents as "a perfect gem," and at his first glance Rymer had agreed with them. The price had been stiff, but at the time Rymer was the possessor of a good-sized fortune. It had taken a third of it to make him the owner of the place and all its fixtures and furnishings, but he had not hesitated.

Aside from the fact that it exactly fulfilled his ideals, he had no intention of settling down, to live on the income which the balance of his money would yield. Not at all.

He decided that he was too young to go on the shelf. He had many ideas for producing further wealth which he intended putting into execution, but he had made up his mind that he would put these ideas into effect in such a way he should not run foul of the law as in the past.

This decision had been arrived at owing to a twofold reason. The first was a real desire to have a permanent place, which he could call his own, and to which he could always return— a place where his neighbours would know nothing of the notorious Dr. Huxton Rymer, and where he could take some part in the social activities of the surrounding countryside.

Then, too, he was still keen on research work, and the place he had bought in Sussex was ideal as a quiet retreat where he could indulge his scientific bent to the full.

Secondly an accidental meeting in London shortly after his arrival in England had convinced him that, if he were to have a permanent stake in England, he would have to carry out his future plans with great precaution.

He had been staying at the Hotel Venetia while the negotiations were in progress for the purchase of Abbey Towers. He had gone down to dinner in the grill-room rather early one evening, intending to go on to a theatre afterwards. As luck would have it, at the very next table sat Sexton Blake, who was dining with a man whom Rymer knew, by sight, as an official of the Foreign Office.

A little to his surprise Blake had bowed, then had gone on with his dinner as though there were nothing at all remarkable in the fact that Rymer was in London, living openly and undisguised at a large hotel. And yet it was less than two months since Blake had been on the other's heels in New York—at the time Rymer had made the clean-up of his present fortune in a big whisky smuggling deal.

Rymer returned the bow and sat down. "If he thinks he is going to make me funk it he is mistaken," he muttered. "He's game, though. I'll say that. He never turned a hair at seeing me walk in, and I fancy I didn't either."

When he had given his order he sat back and lighted a cigarette. He gazed idly about the room, but in reality was watching Blake. He noticed that the latter and the official from the Foreign Office had reached their coffee and liqueurs, and made up his mind they would soon depart. As a matter of fact it was only a few minutes later when they rose.

Then, a little to Rymer's surprise, they parted at the table, and while the Foreign Office man passed out of the grill-room, Blake strolled across and drawing out a chair seated himself at Rymer's table.

"You have returned to England recently?" asked Blake pleasantly.

Rymer nodded, thinking all the time: "Now, I wonder what his game is? Why has he asked me that? And what is he going to lead up to." He said nothing, however.

"Are you remaining long or only passing through?" continued Blake.

"I haven't decided—definitely," responded Rymer warily.

Blake flicked the ash from his cigar. "I don't suppose you would tell me if you had," he remarked coolly. "I just wanted to tell you that, at present, Scotland Yard is not interested in your movements other than to keep a fatherly eye on you when they know your whereabouts. That old matter of a warrant, for a certain affair in France, has been quashed. I don't know if you are aware of that."

"No, I wasn't," confessed Rymer. "I thought—"

"You thought it was still effective?"

"Yes. Why have you told me this?"

"Because I want to warn you. You have chosen to return to England. There is nothing to prevent you doing so now. Nor am I going to advise Scotland Yard of the fact, if you run straight. As long as you do that, you have nothing to fear from me. But if you don't, then I shall act. That is all. You have a chance here, in the country you prefer above all others, to make an effort to retrieve the past. It is up to you whether you do that, or whether you buck the law again. That is why I propose saying nothing unless you force my hand.

"If my calculations are correct"—and here Blake smiled slightly— "you must have got away from New York with a very decent sum of money. As you took that away from those who had made it unlawfully, you are as much entitled to it as they were. It should be enough to enable you to live as I have suggested. With your brains, you should not find it difficult to make it grow into a much larger sum—legitimately. Think it over, Rymer."

With that, Blake had risen, and with another pleasant nod had followed after the man from the Foreign Office. Rymer had watched him go with a curious expression in his eyes.

"Considering what has happened in the past, that was pretty decent of him," he muttered. "I needn't have taken an assumed name after all. I certainly had no suspicion that Scotland Yard had quashed that warrant for my arrest. I wonder what made them do so. Blake could have told me why, but I don't imagine he would have done so. Anyway I have already begun negotiations under the name I have assumed. So I will continue. It may prove wiser in the long run."

And that was the second reason which had determined Rymer to prosecute his plans for the future with the utmost circumspection. It was this fact that, even if he were living under his own name, he need fear nothing from the unwelcome attentions of the police, that filled him with such deep satisfaction as he smoked his after-dinner cigar and gazed about at his surroundings.

It was a little more than three mouths since he had moved into his new home, and every day had been a full one. He was now more or less settled in the way he wished, and had already dropped into the daily routine which he proposed following. While he desired to know and to stand well with his neighbours he had decided to make no bid for social popularity. He would accept invitations and entertain occasionally, but, beyond that, he would not go.

He had bought a couple of horses, and had turned part of the stables into a garage, where he had installed a big touring car and a small runabout, both of which he drove himself. He had a mechanic to keep the cars in order and drive him occasionally.

A groom and a stable-boy looked after the horses—a gardener and a young assistant took care of the grounds, while the housework was done by the gardener's wife and a housemaid, a pretty and exceptionally intelligent girl who had come from London. An extra woman from the village could come in to help when he entertained. That comprised the household.

As for Rymer's habits. He rose about seven, and after a brisk canter of a few miles returned for breakfast at half-past eight. After breakfast he spent half an hour in the grounds with a cigar, then he entered the north wing which led off the library, and which he had had fitted up at considerable expense as a scientific laboratory.

The architect had carried out his scheme with large oriel windows of stained glass, and at some time the big room had evidently been used as a ball-room. But Rymer had had the windows permanently secured, and as an additional safeguard, had fitted strong steel bars to the inside.

A large steel and heavy glass skylight had been built upon the roof, and this gave sufficient light and ventilation for his purpose. A door leading from the north side to the grounds had been fitted with a new and very complicated lock, of which only Rymer had the key. The only other door was that leading to the library, and this had been made as safe as the other.

To fit up that laboratory as his ambition decreed had cost Rymer very close to eight thousand pounds, but he had not begrudged a single penny of the money. There was nothing finer in all Europe, and there was nothing of recent discovery which had not been incorporated in it. It was a place to bewilder the layman, but a realm of delight to the scientist.

On the right had been installed a large electric furnace for heavy crucible work, while near it was a smaller one for ordinary experiments. Farther along on the same side was a tangle of wires and instruments, armatures and coils and discs where the wireless telegraph and wireless telephone instruments had been erected.

Through the skylight at the top went the aerials.

The wireless telegraph had a listening-in radius of about a thousand miles at night, with a sending power of about six hundred.

The telephone was effective for a distance of a hundred and sixty miles by test; but Rymer had ideas of a new transformer which he hoped would increase that to five hundred.

In the far corner, on the right hand side, was a huge steel cabinet fitted with a combination lock like a safe. In this was his stock of chemicals, acids, poisons, and a collection of the rarest and most expensive drugs and materials for research, that could be got together. In the middle of the room was an enormous glass-topped table made in two sections, one which he intended using for vivisection work, and the other for chemical tests.

On the left side as one entered, was an ordinary laboratory table with glass shelves and cupboard above. Next to that, was a large switchboard covered with gleaming brass plugs and sockets, and which was connected with the electrical apparatus on the opposite side of the room. Close beside it was a vulcanised rubber table on which were several keys, not unlike those used by telegraph operators.

On the wall above was a small brass disc marked like a compass, and on which, a slender needle pointed to the zenith. This was one of the very newest of modern discoveries, and it was one that Rymer guarded with the greatest care. An ordinary electrical heating-stove was beyond that again and, in the far corner, was a heap of spare electrical fittings and parts, test tubes and retorts in cases, brass rods and extra cubicles, and a score of other articles, all of which would eventually find some part in the work of the laboratory.

It was here that Rymer spent his mornings from the time he had finished his after-breakfast cigar, until the little bell, rung by the housemaid pressing an electric button in the library, told him lunch would be ready in half an hour.

After lunch he went out into the grounds again, but on these occasions, he invariably made his way to a small concrete building that had been erected in a thick grove of trees, close to the bank of the stream on the northern side of the estate. Like the keys of the laboratory, Rymer also kept in his own care the key of this building.

His afternoon visit was one of inspection.

Inside the building was an exceptionally powerful engine which ran a delicate but extraordinarily effective dynamo. It was this dynamo which furnished the power to light the house in the summer, and heat it as well in the winter. It also gave him the necessary power for the various needs of the laboratory, and also for the running of several weird-looking machines and delicate lathes, which he had erected in the wing on the south side of the house.

In a small annex of concrete adjoining the engine-house was a pump, which supplied the house and stables with water, and there, too, were a score of exceptionally large storage batteries which left him a surplus at all times, no matter how heavy had been the drain on the power.

The engine itself was controlled by a switch in the laboratory, and another in the wing on the south side. From either of these places he could start and stop the engine at will; by an electric starter, but he always made it a point to devote half an hour after lunch to an inspection of the engine and the batteries.

From the engine-house he would make his way to the wing on the south side, which he had turned into an elaborate workshop. He had not taken the pains to secure the windows and doors as strongly as those of the north wing. But the lathes and machines within were the best and latest that money could buy. There were also copper and nickel baths arranged in parallel rows, and along each side were long work benches containing vices and half-finished tools.

An instrument maker would have recognised it at the first glance as a beautifully equipped miniature workshop for the manufacture of delicate tools, and that is exactly what it was. There, Rymer spent each afternoon until tea-time, fashioning the most delicate types of surgical instruments, which were entirely the work of his own hands, from the first rough grinding, to the final nickelling and polishing.

The output of his miniature factory was, of necessity, limited, but, as soon as each instrument was completed, it was eagerly purchased by a leading dealer of fine surgical instruments in Wimpole Street, whose business it was to supply the exacting surgeons of that aristocratic neighbourhood of the medical profession.

It is no wonder that his output was so sought after, for Dr. Huxton Rymer himself had been one of the finest surgeons who had ever wielded a knife, and his knowledge of just what was required for the most delicate work, was unsurpassed. But little did the surgeon who treasured these beautifully-made instruments dream that they were the manufacture of that once famous surgeon.

In all his dealings with the instrument firm Rymer used the name he had adopted on coming to Abbey Towers—Professor Andrew Butterfield. And, even then, he insisted that the firm keep secret its source of supply.

It was work that he really loved and the income from that (for the instruments sold at very high prices), together with what he made by his scientific writings, and that which he received from his investments, would have enabled him to live very comfortably indeed at Abbey Towers if he had chosen to do so.

After tea it was his custom to devote a couple of hours to his correspondence and writing. The former consisted principally of interesting letters on scientific subjects from other scientists with whom Rymer had opened up correspondence since coming to Abbey Towers, while the latter was the composition of scientific data for the articles which he had begun writing for one of the leading scientific journals.

A brisk circuit of the grounds before dinner, and then, after a cigar, back to work in the laboratory. That rounded off the day, and not even Sexton Blake could have found fault with the routine if that had been the full catalogue.

There were, of course, variations to this programme, such as when Rymer drove into Horsham in the runabout or up to London in the big touring car. Also he had dined out a few times in the neigbourhood, but, so far, had not done any entertaining himself. He thought it wisest to go slow in that direction, and to establish for Professor Andrew Butterfield, a reputation for being genial and a desirable neighbour, but slightly austere and very much wrapped up in his work. And he was succeeding admirably in his objects.

Rymer's substantial contribution to church funds and the vicar's tongue had served to do this. Altogether he was distinctly pleased with the course of things on this evening as he sat after a well-cooked and well-served repast, reviewing the events of the past few weeks.

The entrance of the pretty housemaid caused him to glance up.

"All right, Mary," he said genially. "I am just leaving. You can clear away at once. And by the way, you might set out the decanter and glasses in the library early—I am expecting a visitor during the evening. He is motoring down from London and will probably leave late so you needn't wait up. I will see to the doors."

"Very well, sir," answered the maid in a pleasant voice, and with a remarkably good accent. "Shall I leave supper in the library as usual?"

Rymer nodded as he rose.

"Yes, but make it for two instead of one."

He watched her for a moment as she went about her work in a neat and efficient manner. Then he opened the door and passed along the oak-furnished hall to the porch which led on to the drive. He strolled down the drive for a little way, then, turning to the right, swung off through the miniature park.

It was a lovely evening in late May and the day was just fading. Through the lacy tops of the trees to the west, he could see the rose and pink and mauve streamers of the sun, which had slipped beneath the horizon. In the east, over the downs, the sky was already deepening to purple. A belated chirp sounded here and there among the trees, and a faint breath of wind stirred the blooms of the nearby garden into little bowing rows of fragrance.

But while Rymer was subconsciously drinking in the beauty of it all, his conscious thoughts were on the housemaid he had left back in the dining-room.

"An efficient girl," he muttered, "a very efficient girl. She is neat, quick and more than ordinarily intelligent. Her accent, too, is noticeable. She puzzles me just a little. I wonder just how far I could trust her if it ever became necessary to do so."

And as she rapidly cleared away the remains of dinner her thoughts drifted in the same direction.

"I would like to know a little more of what goes on inside his mind," she soliloquised. "He doesn't think of his scientific pursuits all the time. I am positive of that. He is clever all right, and he has the most sensitive hands I have ever seen, and I saw a few when I was nursing in France. They are the hands of an artist or a great surgeon. There is nothing of the absent-minded bespectacled professor about him. He is extremely up to date in everything. He is distinctly a man of the world, in the real sense and is altogether too young to bury himself down here just to dig into scientific puzzles. I think I am going to find my first position as a housemaid decidedly interesting, if only in the study of my master."

She laughed softly then, and departed for the kitchen.

Rymer would have been even more puzzled had he been able to

guess the form of her thoughts, for, after all, the unspoken wording of them was a little unusual for one of her class. But he didn't know that, and as he heard the sound of a car on the distant road, he started back for the front porch.

A few minutes later a black limousine came up the drive and drew up beside him. From it stepped a thin-faced, good-looking young man who drew off a pair of pale coloured antelope gloves as he advanced to greet his host. He shook hands with Rymer, but did not greet him by name until the car had driven on towards the garage. Then he said:

"Well, Doc, I am right on time you see."

Rymer smiled.

"Since it was your appointment that was your duty. I gather from your letter that your business is urgent. If I am mistaken, then let us not go in for a few minutes."

"It is urgent, but not so urgent as all that. By all means let us remain outside for a while. You have a fine little place here, Doc."

"It is small but ideal for my work. It is quiet, too. Come this way. We can reach the stream from here and come back on the other side. How is everything with you, Jordan?"

The young man shrugged.

"Things might be worse. I should have come to see you before, but I had no idea you were tucked away down here." Then he shot a glance at Rymer. "Is it true, what I hear from several sources, that you are out of the game?"

Rymer nodded.

"Quite true!"

"You have made a big clean-up."

"Not so bad."

"I hear, too, that the Yard and you are like the lion and the lamb."

Rymer laughed.

"Something like that," he admitted.

"Well, I came down for some advice, Doc. I understand that, although you have quit yourself, you are willing to advise others."

"In selected cases I might," responded Rymer coolly. "So that is why you have come down, is it? I rather fancied so. Well here we are back at the house. Come into the library, Jordan, and let me hear your case. We shall then see if it is one that interests me."

With that Rymer tossed away the end of his cigar, and led the way into the house by the side porch. The housemaid was just leaving the library as they entered.

CHAPTER 2. The Thousand Pounds Fee—Rymer Plans the Scoop on Conditions—The Secret Codes—The Woman Who Watched.

AS he closed the door after his guest, Rymer noticed that it was evidently the housemaid's duties that had brought her into the room, for on a table by the fireplace was a tray containing a decanter of whisky and some glasses. Although it was a warm spring evening outside, the maid had lighted a small fire in the grate, knowing that her master would wish it.

Although of robust physique, Rymer had spent so many years in the tropics that, not until summer had really established its rule, could he dispense with a fire in the harsher climate of the north. Although it was still pale dusk outside, the maid had drawn the curtains and turned on the lights, and altogether the room looked very cosy and cheerful.

Jordan gazed about him appreciatively. The "Doc.," as Rymer was known to a few of the inner circle of the numerous strata of society in which Jordan was persona grata, had indeed done well for himself, decided the young man. Rymer had drawn up two easy chairs to the fire, and had hospitably poured out a couple of drinks. Then he pushed a box of cigars across to his visitor, and said:

"Now then, Jordan, let me hear what it is."

The younger man lighted his cigar carefully, and, settling back in his chair, blew a smoke ring into the still atmosphere of the room.

"I am up against it, Doc., and that is why I have come to see you."

"Who told you to come to me?"

"Must I tell you?"

His bearded host nodded curtly.

"It was Palmer. He said he had consulted you about two weeks ago."

"That is true. I am still waiting to hear the result of my—advice."

"I don't know anything about that. I only know that he hasn't pulled off his deal yet."

"Let me hear your own case."

"Well, it's this way, Doc. As you know, I did pretty well over a certain affair last year. Then, on top of that, I was lucky enough to back the winner of the Derby, and collected a nice little packet of winnings. Ferguson and I have been running in half sections together lately, and we are both just about at the limit of funds.

"What I have come to see you about is more Ferguson's suggestion than mine. He went across to New York three weeks ago, on a deal we thought we might be able to pull off there, but there was nothing doing. I had a long letter from him, written from New York. I should say that he took most of our remaining funds with him when he went. Well, he used them all practically; just had enough left to pay his way back, and he is on his way now. He wrote me that he would try to get a line on something on board.

"That was the last I heard from him until I received a wireless message yesterday. As I have said, the scheme is more his than mine, and as it is a little out of my line—you know I have confined myself more or less to mining promotions—I decided, after a conversation with Palmer, that I would ask your advice. That is why I wrote to you yesterday. Palmer gave me the address."

As Jordan paused Rymer nodded, then said:

"Continue, but please be as explicit as you can."

"I will. Firstly, let me say that Ferguson's wireless was sent to me in a private code, which we had arranged to be used, regarding the deal which took him to New York. It will perhaps simplify what I am going to say if I read you the translation of it." As he spoke, the young man took from his pocket a folded piece of paper, and, opening it, began to read. "It runs like this," he said:

"Macmac Courtlandt on board with Courtlandt jewels. Only remaining London two days. Anything on board impossible, as jewels in care purser. Only able ascertain staying Hotel Venetia. Has booked suite by wireless. Try arrange something your end."

As he finished reading and looked up, Rymer asked:

"What does the first word, 'Macmac,' mean? The rest I can understand, as it is all decoded, but not that word."

"That is our code word for Mrs. In our private code, 'Mac' means 'Mr.,' and 'Macmac' means 'Mrs.' Of course, Ferguson had to write the name Courtlandt in full, as we have no code to cover proper names. That is why he used the code prefix. Of course, all the other words, with the exception of the second use of 'Courtlandt' came in code."

"I see. I take it, from the message, that he means to convey the information that Mrs. Stuyvesant Courtlandt, the wife of the well-known New York millionaire, is on board the same steamer by which your friend Ferguson is crossing?"

"Exactly."

"Also, I take it that he means she is bringing across with her the famous Courtlandt jewels, which she has placed in care of the purser?"

"Yes, and those jewels—"

Rymer raised his hand. "My dear fellow, please don't try to tell me anything about the Courtlandt jewels. I catalogued them some years ago. I know all about them. They have been built up from half the collections of Europe and Asia. They are worth anything—anything. I take it that Mrs. Courtlandt is going to enter society in London and Paris with a vengeance, if she is bringing those jewels with her. To my knowledge, it is the first time Courtlandt has allowed them to be brought across. He is a shrewd man, and, you can take it from me, he knows half a hundred brains have schemed for years to get possession of them."

"I know that. I didn't know so much about them yesterday, but after I received Ferguson's wireless I made inquiries in certain quarters. I was told just what you have now said."

"More than that, from what I know of Courtlandt, not only would he insure them for an enormous amount, but I shouldn't be surprised if he had arranged for his wife to be shadowed in Europe by a secret service man to protect them. That is why I think you and Ferguson are tackling a very big deal if you try to get possession of the Courtlandt jewels."

"I realise that, but what am I to do? Ferguson has fallen down. He has tipped me off, and will expect me to have some plan ready when he lands."

"By what steamer is he crossing?"

"The Bretonic."

"Then your friend is right in concluding that he can't get possession of them on board. The Bretonic has a safety deposit vault on board, as strong as any City vault one could find. And you say Mrs. Courtlandt has booked rooms by wireless at the Venetia?"

"Yes. She remains in London only two days. I presume she will go to Paris for clothes, and return to London some time before Ascot."

"That sounds extremely probable unless she expects to take a

14

house in London."

"I hadn't thought of that."

"You will have to think of every detail, if you expect to pull off a thing as big as this successfully."

"Well Doc., what about it? Can't you lay out a plan of campaign for us?"

Rymer smoked thoughtfully for a few minutes. "If I hadn't given up that sort of thing, I should feel strongly inclined to have a shot at it myself," he said slowly. "I planned once to get the Courtlandt collection, but it was too well guarded by Stuyvesant Courtlandt. If they had ever been brought across the Atlantic before I should certainly have done so. However," and he sighed, "I am strictly out of the game."

"Won't you join in with us?" asked Jordan eagerly. "With you I am sure we could pull it off. And there would be quite enough for all of us."

"Nothing doing. I told you I was out of the game, and I am—for the present at least. If I advise you, it will be on a strictly business basis. That is the nearest I propose going to active participation in anything of that sort. And if I do advise you, there are certain conditions which it will be necessary for you to observe. If you agree to these conditions, and, if I do advise you, your success or your failure is your own affair. But, whether you succeed or fail, you forget quick who laid your plan of campaign for you—do you understand?" And as he spoke Rymer's bearded jaw stuck out in an ugly way. "Because if you don't," he went on, "you will find that I shall strike, and strike hard."

"I know—Palmer told me. I am ready to abide by your conditions, if you will advise us."

"Then that is settled. This case interests me sufficiently to do so. After I have named my conditions, and you have agreed to them, I shall see what I can do about a plan. The conditions are these:

"Firstly. It is understood that you have consulted me on a purely hypothetical case; that once I have sketched a plan and assisted you in every way, covered by that understanding, my connection with the matter ceases entirely. Do you agree?"

"I do."

"Secondly. That if the business is brought to a successful conclusion, you dispose of the proceeds through a man whose name I shall write on a piece of paper. Do you agree?"

"I do,"

"Thirdly. That if the business results unsuccessfully, and if you or your associates fall into the clutches of the law, in no way whatsoever shall my name be associated with the matter, or brought into touch with it. That is the most important clause of all. Do you agree?"

"I do."

"Fourthly. Before I formulate a plan of campaign for you, you deposit with me the sum of one thousand pounds in currency notes as a fee. This amount is to cover all services rendered by me, no matter what expense I may be put to in rendering them. It is also a tangible sign that my connection with the affair is finished, beyond any dealings I may have with the man through whom you will dispose of any proceeds, and which would have nothing to do with you. Do you agree?"

"I do."

"Then, let us get to business. I shall make a study of the case, and advise you to the best of my ability. You can either take or leave the plan I shall outline. I shall, of course, work on the theory that it is possible to get possession of anything, if you use sufficient determination and brains to do so. I am not asking you for any written agreement. I think you will find it wise to keep your part of it. If you don't, I shall deal with you. Now then, have you brought the amount of your fee?"

For the first time for several minutes Jordan smiled.

"Yes," be said, "Palmer told me the amount you would require. I don't wonder you have given up active work if you get a single fee of this size. He also told me, it would be useless to bring bank-notes or a cheque—that you insisted on ordinary treasury notes. Here they are. I think you will find the amount correct."

As he spoke the young man took out from several pockets, where he had distributed their bulk, five packets of treasury notes which he tossed across to Rymer. Rymer took them, but did not count them. Rising, he went to a small, but very modern safe, and after working at the combination for a few minutes, opened the door. Jordan, who was watching him saw with amazement how thick the door was. Rymer tossed the bundles of notes inside, and closing the door, gave the knob a twirl.

"That is some safe you have," remarked Jordan.

"It is the newest thing known," answered Rymer carelessly, as he poured out fresh drinks.

"It is guaranteed to resist even the blowpipe and stelasite for ten hours. Now then, Jordan, let us get the facts in sequence.

"To begin with we have the fact that Mrs. Stuyvesant Courtlandt is on board the Bretonic, and, if your message from Ferguson is to be trusted, she is bringing with her the bulk, if not all of the famous Courtlandt jewels, which all the world knows are practically without price. That would be easy enough for Ferguson to discover, for I imagine, no matter how quiet Courtlandt would try to keep that fact, it would leak out and the American papers would be bound to make a big headline of it. The next step is to find out when the Bretonic is due at Plymouth, for of course she will touch there first. Just a moment."

Rymer rose, and walking across to a beautiful wide mahogany desk, which stood near the window embrasure, he took out one of several newspaper files which hung in a tall rack beside the desk. Returning to his seat he sat down, remarking as he did so:

"Before we proceed further, we will look up the 'Movements of Steamers,' and see when the Bretonic is due. Ah, here we are. Bretonic sailed from New York on the nineteenth and is due with American and Canadian mails at Plymouth to-morrow. Now then, let us see if we can get the exact time. Yes, here we are down in the detailed notices. The Bretonic will dock at half-past three in the afternoon, and after the luggage has been passed through the customs, a boat special will leave Plymouth for London arriving at Euston at half-past nine in the evening. That means it will be about ten o'clock before Mrs. Courtlandt reaches the Venetia.

"Now then, the question is, will she give her jewels into the safekeeping of the hotel office, on her arrival, or will she wait until the morning? On that point breaks the whole thing. Now, I know from experience, that it is unusual for a guest to place valuables in the safekeeping of a hotel office at that hour of the night, firstly because the head cashier usually goes off duty about eight o'clock in the evening, and the night cashier is always chary of taking on that sort of responsibility.

"Secondly, the average person thinks that their valuables will be all right for one night if they arrive late, as they count on no one knowing of them so soon. At any rate, the plan I outline is going to be based on that assumption."

Rymer abruptly laid the file on the floor and turned to Jordan.

"What time did you receive the wireless message from Ferguson? And have you any idea what time it was despatched from the ship?"

"Yes. It was despatched at nine-twenty in the morning. I received it at a few minutes after eleven. I ran into Palmer about noon, and, after talking to him, wrote you at once."

"Then it was sent while the Bretonic was well off Ireland. Now, if she is arriving at Plymouth at half-past three to-morrow afternoon, it means she is somewhere south-west of Ireland to-night. All right. Come along to my laboratory. I am going to send a message through to Ferguson to-night."

"Send a message through to Ferguson tonight!" exclaimed Jordan in amazement. "What on earth do you mean, Doc?"

"Wait and see," responded Rymer. "But before you come into the laboratory throw that cigar away. No smoking allowed there at present. I have some dangerous stuff under experiment."

Utterly mystified, Jordan followed his host across the room to where a heavy pair of curtains hung between two bookcases. Thrusting these aside, Rymer disclosed a big door which he proceeded to unlock. When he had opened it he reached his hand inside and turned a switch. Immediately the great laboratory was flooded with brilliant light, and Jordan gave another gasp. Rymer motioned him into the room, then closed the door and locked it. He strode across the room to the vulcanized-rubber table which supported the wireless telegraph outfit. Seating himself, he lifted a delicate set of auriculars and fitted them on his head. Then, as his fingers rested on a switch which would throw the whole system into effective function, he said:

"Sit down, Jordan. I will show you how I am going to send a message through to Ferguson to-night."

Jordan, who was beginning dimly to comprehend what Rymer intended doing, seated himself on a small, rubber-protected stool. Rymer reached for a thin volume, which lay on a shelf above the sending apparatus, it was a detailed code of all station and ship wireless calls registered throughout the world. He ran his eye down the index until he came to the section covering the Crescent Line.

Taking a pencil from his pocket, he jotted down the code call of the Bretonic as well as the code call of a land office of origin; then he pressed a switch and a low deep humming sound broke out as the current came on. As his fingers hovered over the sending key he said:

"If the operator at the sending-office whose code I am going to use, ever compares notes with the operator on the Bretonic, there is going to be a slight argument, I fancy. But, in any event, the operator at the sending-office won't spot my call to-night?"

"Why?" asked Jordan with interest.

"Because I am using a different note, and it will only break in on him with a rumble. Even if he does spot it, he won't do so before I get the message through, and he won't he able to tell where it comes from. I shan't give him time to locate direction or distance, either by the antenna or triangle test.

"I have no idea what wave length the Bretonic operator works on, but most of the passenger and commercial boats work on six-hundred metres, so I will start with that. I may have to tune up some other wave length, but I shall soon be able to tell. In the meantime, I want you to put this message in the code which you and Ferguson use."

As he finished speaking, Rymer picked up a pencil and began writing a message in ordinary English on the pad which he always kept on the desk by the sending board. It read as follows:

"Book by wireless room at Hotel Venetia. Will meet you at Euston on arrival of boat train to-morrow night. If possible discover what floor Mrs. Courtlandt requested and book same floor."

Jordon took the slip of paper which Rymer tore from the pad and, after reading it over, nodded his head. "That will be easy to put into code except for the name 'Courtlandt' and 'Venetia' which will have to go in plain words. But what is the idea, Doc?"

"I will tell you later. Get it into code for me. I am going to try to get the Bretonic now on the six-hundred metre wave length."

With that Rymer pressed his finger on the key and a vicious spitting of blue flame followed as he sent through the calm night the code call: "XC—XC—XC!" over and over again.

After a bit he paused, and bending his head and closing his eyes, so as to shut out all objects which might distract his attention, he listened.

He could hear sounds on the same wavelength to which he was tuned up; but, after a little, discovered that they had no relation to the call he was trying to get through. For some time he kept at it on the six-hundred metre length, then he desisted, and tuned up to a thousand metres. Suddenly he detected a response, and, after a repetition of the call, got the reply for which he was waiting.

He made a sign to Jordan that he was through to the Bretonic, and Jordan passed across the slip of paper, on which he had written the private code of the message Rymer had made out. Then Rymer started tapping out the message, while the big drum above his head spat blue flame in a flashing jumble of shorts and longs. When the operator on the Bretonic had signified that he had got it, Rymer listened in for a little while.

It was less than five minutes before he heard some other station calling the Bretonic, and with a smile he closed the switch, shutting off the power. As he removed the phones from his ears he turned to Jordan and said:

"It went through all right, but some other station is calling the Bretonic now. It is possibly the one whose signal I used. But, unless he has been in touch with the ship this evening, I don't think so. He is not likely to be tuned up to the thousand metre length on which the Bretonic is working. It is more likely another ship of the Crescent Line calling. Anyway, it was a risk I had to take. Even if the thing is spotted, they won't be able to trace it now."

"Do I take it, then, Doc, that the sending of this wireless message to Ferguson means you have a plan of campaign ready for us?"

"Certainly. You sought my professional advice, didn't you? And I have accepted your fee, haven't I? Then that is sufficient. Before you leave here to-night you will be in full possession of a plan which, in my opinion, should be a reasonable scheme for getting possession of Mrs. Stuyvesant Courtlandt's jewels. I cannot say, of course, what complications may arise. That is for you and your partner to dispose of. As I remarked before, the plan I have formulated is based on the assumption that Mrs. Courtlandt will keep her jewels in her room on the first night of her arrival in London.

"If, on the other hand, she insists on giving them into the safe keeping of the hotel that first night, then my scheme falls to the ground, and you will have to return for another plan. That I shall, of course, furnish without any further fee. But if you follow my instructions, and don't lose your nerve, I don't think the lifting of the jewels should be at all a matter of impossibility. Now, then, I shall explain some of the points.

"Firstly, we have the arrival of Mrs. Courtlandt at the Venetia at about ten o'clock tomorrow night. She will be accompanied, no doubt, by a maid; and, as I remarked, it is just possible that up to the time of her arrival at the hotel she may be under the care of a private detective, sent by Courtlandt to watch over the jewels. Once she has arrived there, however, and has gone to her rooms, his vigilance is bound to be relaxed.

"If such a person does exist, then he will probably also have a room, in the hotel. We will assume that Mrs. Courtlandt will be tired on her first night, and will retire early. The maid will do only the unpacking that is absolutely necessary, and will probably complete it the following day, when her mistress is not in the apartments.

"However, to-morrow you will be able to discover by the plan I shall outline exactly what apartment has been booked for Mrs. Courtlandt, and, after that, you must pass it and discover just how the rooms are situated. I fancy it will be on either the first or second floor. Most of the apartments on those two floors of the Venetia give either on to the large central court of the hotel, or on to Piccadilly.

"My scheme is based on these presumptions, and that is why I have also wirelessed to Ferguson to book a room at the hotel. With two of you in different rooms, you will have a double chance of securing one which will be suitable enough to put the plan into effect. Also, I am going to give you an alternative plan—that is, one plan will be based on the possibility that you will be compelled to work from the corridor outside her room, and the other on the chance that you may find it more convenient to work either from a room above or a room beneath one of those composing her apartment.

"Now listen carefully to what I am going to say. Afterwards I shall explain in detail the use of the appliances, with which I shall furnish you, for the purpose you have in mind."

Then Rymer began speaking in low, careful tones, and as he unfolded the scheme Jordan's eyes lit up with excitement. And when, nearly an hour later, Rymer had finished, the other felt perfectly satisfied with the stiff fee which Rymer had charged.

Another half-hour was spent by Rymer explaining, very carefully, the exact means of using the appliances, which he was supplying gratis along with his advice. When Jordan had demonstrated that he quite understood their use, they made their way back to the library, where the housemaid had laid a tray containing supper for two.

At a little after midnight Jordan started on his drive back to London. His plans were now crystallised, and in a small, plain leather bag at his feet were the appliances with which Rymer had provided him, and by the scientific ingeniousness of which Jordan hoped to pull off the great "job" successfully.

Back in the library at Abbey Towers, Professor Andrew Butterfield mixed himself a whisky-and-soda; then, seating himself at his desk, began to elaborate a particularly abstruse point in the article on blood pressure which he was writing for a leading medical journal.

At the same time the window curtains of an upper room were pushed aside, and the efficient housemaid of the Towers, who ought to have been in bed long ago, followed the course of the lights of Jordan's car as it went down the drive and turned towards Horsham.

CHAPTER 3.   A Bolt from the Blue— Tinker's Strange Report —The 'Phone Call from London—The Famous Courtlandt Jewels.

TINKER lightly vaulted the wooden fence which separated the open meadow from the plantation, and, whistling cheerfully, made his way along the quiet, dew-dripping path towards the house. It was still only a little after seven o'clock, and, although the sun was already well above the horizon, its heat had not yet been sufficient to dissipate the heavy dew which had fallen in the night. Tinker had been out since six o'clock, and had covered a good five miles across country, and now he was returning to the house with an appetite sharp on edge.

He and Blake had been down in Kent now for a few days, staying at a lovely old country place which had been lent to Blake by young Lord Ranborough, who was in Norway on business.

Both Sexton Blake and Tinker had had a pretty strenuous winter and spring, and when Ranborough had popped into the consulting-room in Baker Street and had casually dropped some keys on Blake's desk, with the remark that he was off that day for Norway and the house would be at Blake's disposal for a month, Blake had laughed, and, after some argument, had finally accepted. Thus it came that they were at Ranborough Hall, in Kent, and hoped to remain there until well into June.

Usually Blake accompanied Tinker on the morning ramble, but on this particular morning Blake had risen early to make out some urgent telegrams for despatch to London, and Tinker had gone off by himself. The plantation which he had just entered from the open meadow was a small one of about fifty acres, and had been planted some thirty years before.

It lay between the vegetable gardens on the west side of the house, and Tinker had chosen to return that way, as the path would bring him round by the stables where he wanted to have a look at the horses and the kennels before going into breakfast.

He had gone some thirty or forty yards along the narrow path when he paused and glanced up. Just overhead something had crashed in one of the trees, and Tinker's first idea was that he had flushed a bird by the noise of his passage. The next moment, however, his eyes opened wide with astonishment as something large and heavy came crashing down from branch to branch, and finally landed with a dull thud on the soft ground a few feet to his right.

Bending over the object, Tinker examined it, and as he did so his expression became more puzzled than ever. Suddenly an idea came to him, and, racing back along the path, he vaulted the fence into the meadow, and kept on across the open field until he was well clear of the wood. Then he stopped and gazed up into the cloudless, blue sky above. Slowly he turned on his heel, studying the blue towards every point of the compass. All the time he was listening, too, but there was neither sight nor sound of the nature he had expected.

His gaze swept the wood and wandered about his immediate surroundings. But, beyond a lark singing somewhere in the blue above, and the distant sound of somebody chopping, he seemed to be entirely alone in the fresh loveliness of the morning. He shook his head in a puzzled way, and went back slowly towards the wood.

He vaulted the fence again, and walked along to where he had left the strange object that had literally dropped like a bolt from the blue. It still lay where it had fallen. Tinker bent over it again. It took him only a moment to confirm his first impression. The object was a large dressing-case, one that it was easy to see had cost a considerable sum.

It was covered with a loose jacket of heavy canvas, but this, he could see, was but to protect the rich purple morocco leather of which the case was made. On the purple canvas cover the letters "S. C." were stamped in gold. The twin locks were of heavy brass, which Tinker found yielded easily. He pressed them, then lifted the lid of the case.

The inside was lined with purple velvet, and had been fitted with compartments and pouches, covered with the same material. But, as far as he could see, the case was quite empty. Stamped in gold inside the lid was a name, the beginning initials of which Tinker saw were the same as those on the outer cover. The name was "Sophie Courtlandt." Tinker closed the lid and pressed the brass lock catches back into place. Then he picked it up, and continued his way to the house.

Instead of going round to the stables and kennels, he entered by the front way, and went straight to a small study which was situated in the left wing of the mansion, and where he knew he was pretty sure to find Blake. As he surmised, Blake was sitting at a desk, working away at his telegrams. He glanced up as Tinker entered, but apparently thought nothing of the case which the lad was carrying, for he turned back to his work without any remark.

"I say, guv'nor," said Tinker, as he set the dressing-case on the floor, "look what I have found!"

Blake glanced up again, and his gaze rested on the case.

"A dressing-case, eh? Where did you find it, Tinker?"

"In the plantation on my way back to the house. But I say, guv'nor, listen while I tell you how I came across it."

Blake laid down his pencil, and leant back.

"How?" he asked.

"I had just jumped the fence from the meadow, and was coming along the path through the plantation, when I heard a crash in the trees overhead, and, looking up, I saw this case come tumbling down through the branches. I thought that was funny. At first I thought to myself, now, that case has been up in the top branches of one of those trees, and has, just slipped down. But when I bent over it, guv'nor, I found it was perfectly dry, except where it had rubbed against the branches and leaves in falling.

"Well, last night there was a very heavy dew. The grass and trees are still wet. If it had been up in the tree for any length of time, then, it seemed to me, that it ought to be wet with dew all over, which it wasn't. So the next thing I thought was it has fallen from some aeroplane which is flying overhead. So I left it where it had dropped, and ran back along the path to the meadow. I got well out in the open there, and looked up in the sky in every direction. There wasn't either sight or sound of any aeroplane, guv'nor. So I returned to where I left it, and examined it.

"As you can see, it is a very fine case of morocco leather. This canvas cover is just to protect it. It isn't locked either. And there is nothing inside. But you see these initials on the cover, guv'nor, 'S.C.'? Well, that means 'Sophie Courtlandt,' for here is the name stamped in full inside the lid. That must be who owns it. Now who do you suppose she is, guv'nor, and how do you think the case came there in the plantation this morning?"

Blake, who had begun to listen idly to Tinker's relation, showed an increased interest as the lad proceeded, and, when he had finished, Blake said:

"Bring it over to the window, my lad. It is certainly odd finding a thing of this sort in the plantation. And your instinctive deduction about the dew does you credit."

Tinker carried the case across, and, after a cursory glance at the initials on the canvas cover, Blake pressed back the catches, and lifted the lid. He saw that it was just as Tinker had said. The inside was lined with purple and was quite empty, while the name, "Sophie Courtlandt," had been stamped in small gold letters on the inside of the lid.

Blake removed the canvas cover, and, on the outside of the morocco was also stamped the initials "S.C." One corner of the canvas was stained with mud where it had struck the ground, and there were still traces of damp here and there where, as Tinker had said, it had been brushed by the leaves and twigs in falling through the trees.

"Are you quite sure the branches at the top of the tree were not thickly leafed enough to shelter it from the dew, supposing it had been placed on the branches?" he asked after a moment.

"Almost certain, guv'nor. They are quite thin, and everything is dripping still, although the sun has been up some time. The dew was very thick on the plantation last night."

"It is certainly odd, my lad. I don't know of anyone of the name of Courtlandt living in the neighbourhood. But we can ask the butler that. If your theory that it might have dropped from an aeroplane is the explanation, then the machine might have passed overhead very early this morning, before you were abroad. The case might have lodged in the trees and only slipped down as you came along — though I confess that doesn't seem very likely. It is too heavy to remain for long in a precarious position of that kind, and then gradually slip to the ground."

"Well, no machine has passed over since six o'clock," said Tinker. "I was in the open country nearly all the time and I should have been bound to see it, or hear it."

"That is true," rejoined Blake thoughtfully.

"And there is nothing about it to give us a clue either. Beyond the mud on the corner of the cover, the damp on the canvas and this little piece of green cord tied on the handle, there is nothing whatsoever. We know how the damp and the mud came there, and the cord, I fancy, is where a tag has been tied to the handle at some time or other. The name is the one thing we have to go on. Ah! here is the butler. We will ask him if he knows of anyone of this name in the neighbourhood."

A knock had come at the door, and the butler entered, bearing the London papers which had come down by an early morning train. As he laid them on the desk and announced that breakfast was served, Blake made a gesture detaining him.

"Tinker has found this dressing-case in the grounds, Ferris." he said. "The initials on the cover correspond to the name inside— Courtlandt. Do you know of anyone of the name in the neighbourhood?"

The old man shook his head at once. "No, sir. I am quite certain there is no one of that name living near here."

Blake nodded. "It is strange how it came into the grounds. It is of some value, too. If no one calls to inquire about it, I shall put a notice in the paper."

With that he thrust the case to one side and led the way into breakfast. Leaving Tinker to rummage about among the hot dishes on the sideboard and to select his as well as his own, Blake seated himself at the table and opened one of the papers which had just come. He had just begun reading the foreign cables, when a footman entered the room to inform him that he was wanted on the telephone.

With a slight gesture of irritation Blake laid the paper down and rose. The mansion possessed a small switchboard in a little room off the hall with telephone communication to most of the public rooms and bedrooms, but there was no regular operator.

The plug on the board was usually kept into the main circuit, and it was the instrument at this board to which Blake made his way. He discovered that he had been called by Browning, the manager of the Hotel Venetia in London.

When he had assured himself that it was Blake to whom he was speaking, he said:

"I rang up your house, Mr. Blake, and your housekeeper gave me your address. I understand from her that you are having a short holiday and do not wish to be bothered with business, but, as the matter about which I wish to see you is of a serious nature, I took the liberty of calling you on the telephone."

"It will have to be pretty serious to justify that," responded Blake shortly. "My housekeeper gave you the message I left for her to deliver to everyone who desired to see me. What is the trouble?"

"It is difficult for me to go into details over the telephone. Could you possibly come to London to-day?"

"Frankly, Browning, I'd rather not. I haven't had a holiday for several months now, and I don't care about tackling any business until I return to London. If you are in any difficulty why don't you go to Scotland Yard— if it is a police matter?"

"It is a police matter, and I have already notified Scotland Yard. But the managing director has also asked me to consult you. It is a big thing, Mr. Blake."

"Well, what is it? If you can't enter into detail over the telephone, you can at least give me an idea of the nature of the case."

"We have had a robbery in the hotel during the night. It is a very serious matter. One of our guests who arrived from America last night has been robbed of all her jewels. From what I can discover they are of very great value and, naturally, while we are not legally responsible for the loss as they were not placed in our care for safekeeping, we must do all we can to recover them. There is absolutely no indication as to how they were taken. The loss was discovered only an hour ago. I have notified Scotland Yard, and when I informed the managing director he instructed me to consult you at once. I—we should be very grateful if you would make an exception and assist us."

"Who was the guest?" asked Blake shortly.

"Mrs. Stuyvesant Courtlandt, of New York."

"What—you mean the wife of the well-known New York millionaire?"

"Yes. Do you know him?"

"I have met him—yes.—You surely don't mean that she had the Courtlandt jewels with her?"

"I mean just that—or at least she says so."

"Listen!" put in Blake quickly. "Can you tell me her Christian name? If you don't know, make inquiries, and find out if it is Sophie."

"I don't know it, but I can find out in a few moments. Will you hold the line, please."

Blake tapped the table impatiently until he heard Browning's voice again. "Well?" he demanded, as he heard the other's inquiry if he were there.

"You are quite right. Her Christian name is Sophie, Mr. Blake."

"Are you speaking from your private office?"

"Yes."

"Then tell me please, as briefly as possible, exactly what has happened. Never mind about details. Just give me the facts."

"Mrs. Courtlandt arrived at the hotel last night. She crossed from New York on the Bretonic. She sent us a wireless from the ship reserving rooms. We gave her a suite on the second floor. The boat special arrived at Euston about half-past nine, and Mrs. Courtlandt reached the hotel about ten—or a few minutes past. I was not on duty at the time. On her arrival here she made some mention of giving the cashier something for safekeeping; but, on finding that the head cashier had gone off duty, and that the assistant cashier was is charge, she told him she would wait until the morning.

"She went to her rooms at once, where the floor waiter served supper. I had just come on duty this morning, when I was sent for to go to her rooms. I went up at once. She informed me that on her arrival here she had with her a case containing a very valuable quantity of jewels. This case had been placed beside her bed by her maid before she retired. Early this morning Mrs. Courtlandt, who was suffering from a slight cold, woke, and remembering that the maid had left a bottle of aspirin on the dressing-table, got out of bed to get it. It was then that she noticed the case which had been left beside her bed was gone. She looked about the room, then rang for the floor attendant, and sent word to her maid to come immediately. The maid had a room on the top floor. Shortly after, she rang for me to come up, and informed me of what had happened. When I was quite convinced that the case had disappeared, I consulted with the managing director in his private apartment which, as you know, he has in the hotel. He instructed me to notify Scotland Yard, and afterwards to consult you on behalf of the management of the hotel.

"As far as I can discover, the jewels which Mrs. Courtlandt brought with her, were part of a very valuable collection. Detective-inspector Thomas is now interviewing Mrs. Courtlandt. Those are the bare facts, Mr. Blake."

"Was Mrs. Courtlandt's maid the only personal servant who was travelling with her?"

"No. She had also a private male attendant. I did not know about him until this morning. The clerk thought he was a private courier. As a matter of fact, he is an American private detective, who was sent by Mrs. Courtlandt's husband to keep watch on her jewels."

"That is all?"

"Yes—no other servants."

"Very well, Browning. I shall catch a train about nine-thirty for London. It arrives at Charing Cross somewhere about ten-twenty. Please send a car to meet me, as mine is being overhauled, and I don't want to use one of Lord Ranborough's for a journey of this sort."

"Thank you very much, Mr. Blake. I shall have a car at the station waiting for you."

With that Blake rang off and made his way back to the breakfast-room. Tinker had already piled both plates with, what he considered, a very modest beginning for the meal, but which Blake gazed at in dismay.

"Look here, young 'un," he said as he sat down, "if you keep up this early morning stunt of yours, I shall have to ration you."

"Ration me!" exclaimed Tinker. "Why that isn't much, guv'nor. I only served enough as an appetizer. Wait until you see the kidneys and bacon to follow."

Blake groaned in mock horror, causing a footman who hovered about to hide a grin. Nevertheless, Blake found that Tinker had not overestimated as much as he thought, for he demolished nearly everything the lad had piled on his plate. But he did draw the line at the second load which Tinker tried to help him to, contenting himself with the toast and marmalade. When he saw that they needed nothing more, the young footman left the room, and, when the door had closed after him, Blake said:

"Well, my lad, you dropped on to something odder than we thought this morning."

"Do you mean about the dressing-case, guv'nor?" asked Tinker, looking up with interest.

"You don't mean your call on the telephone had something to do with it?"

"Perhaps not to do with the case itself, but certainly to do with the lady who owns it—Mrs. Stuyvesant Courtlandt."

"Was it a 'phone message from the person who lost it, guv'nor?"

"No; and I doubt very much if Mrs. Courtlandt has the remotest idea that her dressing-case was found down here in Kent."

"What do you mean, guv'nor?"

"This, my lad. Mrs. Stuyvesant Courtlandt, the wife of the New York millionaire, Stuyvesant Courtlandt, was robbed last night in the Hotel Venetia, of a great portion of the famous Courtlandt jewels. And, unless I miss my guess, the jewels were in the morocco dressing-case which you found in the plantation this morning."

"Good heavens, guv'nor! Was that what the telephone message was about?"

Blake nodded. "Yes—it was from Browning, the manager of the Venetia."

"That means they want you to take up the case."

"Yes."

"What did you say, guv'nor?"

"I said I would. I am going to town after breakfast. Would you like to come, or would you rather remain here?"

"I'd rather come."

"Very well. You needn't pack much for us. If we stay overnight we can get what we need at Baker Street."

CHAPTER 4. Blake's Arrival at the Venetia—Collecting Together the Facts of the Robbery.

THEY got away from the little village station shortly after nine, and, on reaching Charing Cross, found Browning himself waiting for them with a big limousine. Blake had brought with him the dressing-case which Tinker had found in the plantation, but, at the village station, he had pasted a railway label over the initials, so that Browning, who had never seen the case, did not suspect whose property it really was.

While Blake was quite convinced that the dressing-case must have some bearing on the robbery, he had decided that, for the time being, he would keep its existence secret. He wanted to find out first what conclusions the officers from the Yard had come to, and particularly to discuss the affair with his old friend Detective Inspector Thomas.

On reaching the Venetia, they went along at once to Browning's office, where Blake left the dressing-case and Tinker left the two small bags he had packed for himself and Blake. Then Blake turned to Browning:

"I want first to go to Mrs. Courtlandt's apartment. Can she receive us now?"

"Oh, yes. She has already been interviewed by the men from Scotland Yard."

"Oh, are they still here?"

"I think Inspector Thomas is still here. I told him you were coming up, and he said he would have breakfast here and wait for you."

"All right. Let us go up to the apartment, then."

The manager led the way to the lift, and, on reaching the second floor, led the way along to the apartment occupied by Mrs. Courtlandt. He knocked on the door, which was opened by Mrs. Courtlandt's maid. They found Mrs. Courtlandt clad in a filmy morning wrap with a lacy boudoir cap on her head. Her face showed distinct signs of the shock she had undergone, but she was making feeble attempts to consume a light breakfast which had been served in the room.

Browning introduced Blake and Tinker, and then stood on one side to allow Blake to question her. Her manner was distinctly gracious. Undoubtedly, the fact that the famous criminologist had been staying at Lord Ranborough's place in the country (a fact which Browning had communicated to her) made a considerable impression on her.

"I am so glad you have come, Mr. Blake," she gushed. "I am nearly distracted."

Blake bowed. "And I am very sorry to hear of your loss, Mrs. Courtlandt," he said suavely.

"I quite realise what a shock it must be to you, and also that you have already been questioned by the officers from Scotland Yard. But I must ask you a few questions before I—er— can make any attempt to recover your jewels."

"Oh, they have fatigued me so, these officers," she rejoined wearily. "But please ask me what you wish, Mr. Blake. I am sure you will only ask what is necessary."

Again Blake bowed. "I shall ask you only what is absolutely necessary, Mrs. Courtlandt," he said. "It will perhaps save time if you will tell me everything you can remember about your movements, from the time you arrived at the hotel until you discovered your loss."

She began to do so, and, as she proceeded, Blake noted that in sum and substance it was practically what Browning had told him over the telephone. She described how she had arrived at the Venetia in a car sent by the hotel, which she had telegraphed for from Plymouth, how she had thought of leaving her jewel case in the care of the cashier, but that, on finding only an assistant cashier would be on duty until the morning, she had decided to keep the case in her own room.

Then she related how, after a light supper, her maid had laid out her things and she had prepared to retire. She was a little verbose in describing events up to the time when the maid had finally departed, and how she herself had bolted the doors of the bedroom and the sitting-room before she turned out the lights.

"They were locked, but I bolted them as well," she said. "I was nervous about my jewels, although I didn't really think that anything would happen. I left the light on the night-table on, and it was still on when I woke early this morning. But the case was gone."

"What time was that, Mrs. Courtlandt?"

"A few minutes after six. I have a slight cold, and, on waking, got up to get some aspirin. It was then I noticed the jewel-case was gone."

"Did you notice if the doors were still bolted?"

"Yes—they were just as I had left them."

"Then I take it you intended that your maid should waken you by knocking this morning, and you would let her in yourself?

"No, There is also a door leading from the bathroom on to the corridor. She was to come in that way with the hotel maid's master-key.

"Ah, yes! I hadn't thought of that. That door locks, of course, with the same type of spring lock as the other doors?" This to Browning.

The manager nodded. "Yes; and, as far as the officers from Scotland Yard could make out, it had not been tampered with."

Blake turned back to Mrs. Courtlandt. "And after you made the discovery?"

"After that—why—oh! I looked all about the room. But I knew it had disappeared. It was close beside my bed when I went to sleep, and all my keys were in a little bag under my pillow. They were all right—had apparently not been touched. But while I had slept, someone had entered the room and taken the case."

Had you taken any form of sleeping-draught before retiring?"

"Nothing beyond a glass of hot milk."

"Are you, ordinarily, a heavy sleeper?"

"On the contrary, I sleep very lightly."

"What about the windows? Were they open?"

"The two windows in this room were open, and one window in the bedroom. The bathroom window was closed. It was rather close last night."

Blake nodded, and walked across the sitting-room to one of the windows. He found that it looked out on the great centre court of the hotel, but there was no balcony of any sort outside the room. The sill was about a foot and a half from the floor, and the window was of the ordinary type, with top sash and bottom sash—not French window's. The lower sash was still open a few inches, and Blake raised it to the limit. Then he leant out a little, and gazed upwards and downwards. Apparently there was nothing of particular interest to be seen, for, after a few seconds, he turned back into the room.

"May I go into the bedroom for a few minutes?" he asked.

"Certainly, Mr. Blake. Anything at all that will help you."

Blake and Tinker entered the bedroom, leaving the manager to talk to Mrs. Courtlandt. The room was a large, beautifully furnished apartment, with a sumptuously fitted bed of the French empire style. There were three doors—the one by which they entered the sitting-room, one directly opposite, which Blake guessed rightly led into the bathroom, and one midway in the wall on their left, which gave on to the corridor.

There were two windows on the right, similar to those in the sitting-room. The heavy curtains had been drawn back, and one of them— that on the left—was open as it must have been during the night.

Piled at the foot of the bed were several trunks, and standing on end, open, between the bed and the left-hand window, was one of the big wardrobe trunks of the type carried by a great number of Americans. A maid, whom Blake took to be Mrs. Courtlandt's private maid, was working over this trunk as they entered.

Between the bed and the door leading to the bathroom, was a night table, on which stood a small electric light. Against the wall, on the right as they entered, was a very large duplex wardrobe, the doors of which were now open, and between the two windows was a massive dressing-table—the one, Blake decided, which Mrs. Courtlandt had gone to get the aspirin. The maid turned as they came into the room, and Blake said:

"You are Mrs. Courtlandt's maid?"

"Yes, sir."

"I am trying to assist your mistress to recover her jewels. I should like to ask you a few questions."

"I don't know much about it, sir. I have already told everything I know."

"Quite so. But I should like to question you further. Tell me, please, exactly what you did last night after arriving at the hotel."

"Well, sir, I came on to the hotel with Mrs. Courtlandt. I came up here with her. I ordered her supper for her, and then began to unpack the things she would need for the night. She told me to leave the rest of the unpacking until the morning. When she had finished her supper, I got her things ready. Then I left I went down to the servants' dining-room, where I had some supper, and after that I went to bed."

"How did you leave this apartment?"

"By the bathroom door."

"Did you lock it?"

"No, sir. It locked itself."

"Are you sure you closed it tightly?"

"Yes, sir. I tried it after I closed it. It was locked."

"Is that all?"

"Yes, sir. I know nothing more until Mrs. Courtlandt sent for me this morning."

"Are you the only private servant Mrs. Courtlandt brought with her?"

"No, sir. There is Mr. Williams."

"Who is Mr. Williams?"

"I don't exactly know, sir. He was employed by Mr. Courtlandt to attend to certain matters for the mistress."

"I see. Did he come up to the rooms last night?"

"No, sir. He came on to the hotel with us, and the mistress told him downstairs that there was nothing else for him to do. He went away then, and I didn't see him after."

"Did he stay in the hotel?"

"He had a room here if that is what you mean, sir."

"Yes, that is what I meant. Thank you. And now, will you show me, please, just where Mrs. Courtlandt's jewel-case was placed."

The maid walked round the bed and paused by the night table.

"It was just on the floor here."

Blake merely glanced at the spot, then, with a nod of dismissal to the maid, he proceeded into the bathroom. It was a large, luxuriously fitted place, with a ground glass window, which gave on the inner court of the hotel, and a second door which led out into the corridor. A brief examination of this revealed that it was as the maid had said— the lock was an automatic affair, permitting one to open the door easily enough from the inside, but not from the outside without a key. Blake returned to the bedroom.

"How did you expect to get in this morning?" he asked the maid.

"With the pass key carried by the hotel chambermaid, sir."

Blake and Tinker continued their way to the sitting-room. Mrs. Courtlandt still sat where they had left her, but she was talking to a man whom Blake had not seen before, and who must have entered the apartment while he and Tinker were absent. Mrs. Courtlandt waved her hand towards the newcomer.

"This is Williams," she said. "Mr. Williams is a New York detective sent by Mr. Courtlandt to watch over the jewels which I brought with me. I wish to say, Mr. Blake, that I do not hold Mr. Williams culpable of the slightest negligence in this matter. He strongly advised me last night to leave my jewel-case in the care of the cashier, and it was due to my express instructions that he retired to his room shortly after our arrival here. He had been on duty for a good many hours."

Blake acknowledged the introduction and the comments by Mrs. Courtlandt which followed. Williams, he saw, was a short, stocky man of typical American appearance. He looked a capable, reliant individual, but it was obvious that he was undergoing deep chagrin over the theft of the jewels, which he had been sent specially to Europe to guard.

He glanced a little curiously at the great British criminologist. He had, of course, heard a good deal about Blake in New York, and knew that Blake was a great friend of the ablest of New York detectives, Bryant Kennedy.

"I should like to have a talk with Mr. Williams presently," said Blake, turning to Mrs. Courtlandt. "By the way, have you seen Inspector Thomas of Scotland Yard?" he asked of Williams.

The other answered with a strong American twang,

"Yes. I had a talk with him about half an hour ago. He is downstairs now. I guess he is waiting to see you."

"In that case, Mrs. Courtlandt, I shall go down. There is nothing more I wish to see here at present. But I wish it made possible for me to gain access to these rooms, during the morning, if necessary. If I might make a suggestion, I would say, firstly, that it is of the utmost importance that for the present the news of the robbery be kept from leaking out, and, secondly, it will assist materially in that if you will try to act as though nothing had happened. Do you think you could go out this morning—any shopping or motoring?"

Blake had made his suggestion as he had already judged Mrs. Courtlandt to be a woman of considerable determination of character, and one who would not give way to useless hysteria, even though the loss was enormous from any way of looking at it. Her conduct since her discovery had told him that. And her reply showed that his confidence was justified, for she said:

"If that will assist in the slightest way, Mr. Blake, I am quite ready to do so. It will be a struggle, for the more I think of this affair, the more mysterious does it appear. It is utterly beyond my understanding how anyone could get into these rooms last night without my waking, but, even more so, how my keys were taken from under my pillow without disturbing me. The more I try to reason it out, the more my thoughts move in a vicious circle."

"As far as possible, you must try not to think of how it happened, Mrs. Courtlandt," advised Blake earnestly. "That can do no good at present. I certainly agree with you that the theft has been carried out with a very considerable degree of ingenuity, but cunning as the thieves have been, they may have left some clue which will give us the lead for which we are seeking. As we probe more deeply into all the channels of suggestion which arise, we may come upon that clue when we least expect to do so, and, rest assured, we shall leave no stone unturned to follow it to its true end."

"I am sure I hope so, Mr. Blake. Mr. Courtlandt would be very upset if he knew, and I am worried about that. Outside of the actual value of the jewels, which is considerable, as you know, they are very rare from the collector's point of view."

"I would not cable him yet," said Blake. "Let us wait a day or two at least. And now, if you will get ready to go out, I will go down and talk to Inspector Thomas."

The whole party, Blake, Tinker, Williams, and Browning, the hotel manager, descended to the ground floor, and proceeded along a narrow corridor to the latter's office. Browning then sent a page to ask Inspector Thomas to come along. The man from Scotland Yard appeared a few minutes later, and, after greeting Blake and Tinker, said:

"Well, Mr. Blake, what do you make of it? I heard you had been called in, and I wanted to compare notes with you."

Blake smiled. He and Inspector Thomas had been mixed up in a good many cases together in the past, and he knew the inspector for one of the ablest men at the Yard.

While their methods were radically different, the inspector had a very deep respect for the scientific process by which Blake applied logic and deduction to a case, and, on more than one occasion, the criminologist had gratuitously given him a strong lead which had placed a solution in his hands, and had considerably enhanced his standing at the Yard. Years before, when he had first run across the young scientist who was just down from university, he had looked upon his methods as the useless play of an amateur, but the inspector had acquired wisdom since those days.

He had long since thrown off the attitude of superior officialdom, adopted by so many Yard men in the presence of the unorthodox investigator.

"What do you make of it yourself, inspector?" he asked. "You were first on the scene, and, also, you have had a talk with Mr. Williams."

Inspector Thomas shook his head warily.

"I am not committing myself to anything definite yet," he replied. "But as far as I have gone it looks like an inside job to me—although that doesn't say much in the case of a public hotel."

Blake walked across to the corner where he had deposited the dressing-case, which had appeared so mysteriously that morning, several miles away in Kent. While Inspector Thomas gazed at the sight in dumb amazement, Blake laid it on the desk and gestured for Williams to examine it.

"Will you just confirm, Mr. Williams, whether this is Mrs. Courtlandt's dressing-case or not?"

The New York detective, with an expression that rivalled that of the inspector, did as Blake asked. After a cursory study of both the exterior and the interior, he glanced up at Blake.

"It is Mrs. Courtlandt's case all right," he said slowly. "And it is the case which contained her jewels. Do you mind telling me where you got this, Mr. Blake? '

"Presently," responded Blake. "Had Mrs. Courtlandt any other dressing-case similar to this?"

"No."

"Then there can be not the slightest doubt that this is the one in which she had packed the jewels?"

"Not the slightest."

"Then we may safely take it that this is the case which was taken from her last night. Now you will notice that the locks have not been broken, nor has the case been cut or defaced in any way. That bears out Mrs. Courtlandt's statement that the keys were taken from beneath her pillow while she slept. There is only one reason for the thief or thieves taking such a risk as that—they were determined not to make any mistake. While they may have thought the jewels were in this case, they didn't want to run the risk, after they got away, of finding that they had been fooled. They, apparently, did not bother to relock it and 'take' the key with them, but left it as we see it now. Where they abstracted the jewels we don't know yet, but 1 can tell you where they got rid of this case."

"Where?" asked the inspector eagerly.

"About forty miles from here—in Kent," said Blake. "But I will let Tinker tell you about that. It was he who found it."

For the next five minutes all interest was centred upon Tinker, who, brought thus into the limelight by Blake, related tersely and succinctly how the dressing-case had appeared so mysteriously out of the dead blue dome of the morning sky. When he had finished, Inspector Thomas wagged his head sagely.

"That's easy," he said. "But it complicates matters considerably."

"Exactly how do you mean?" asked Blake.

"Why, isn't it plain enough? The job was pulled off during the night, some time. The thief or thieves got away with the haul, and made for some spot where they had an aeroplane waiting. They are probably somewhere on the Continent by now, and on the way they took the jewels from the case and dropped that over the side. I have already sent out the word to have every port watched, but I never counted on them escaping by aeroplane."

Blake nodded slowly, and lighted a cigarette.

"Possibly you are right, inspector," he said. "But it should not be so difficult to test your theory. If the thieves went by aeroplane, then it should not be impossible to trace their point of leaving.

"They must have had a starting-place near, London, and aeroplane traffic is so general these days, that all authorised journeys are as easy to catalogue as those of an express train. And that is just why an unscheduled flight would be noticed by someone. But before your thieves could make such an escape they had to leave the hotel.

"Now then, supposing we assume that your theory is right? In that case the aeroplane must have crossed over Lord Ranborough's place in Kent, somewhere between five and six in the morning. That means it would have to leave London, or whatever spot near London from which the flight was started, at, say, any time between four and five.

"In other words, I give the machine an hour between the starting-point and its passage over Lord Ranborough's place. Very well. Then let us say that they couldn't have started from an aerodrome, either public or private, nearer than Hendon, or, perhaps, Croydon. The cross-Channel flying companies allow exactly an hour, from the point in London where they pick up passengers, for the motor journey to Croydon; and it takes a little under that time to get to Hendon.

"Let us assume that, with ordinary delays, the thieves took an hour to get to the point where the aeroplane was waiting. That puts the time when they would have to leave the hotel at between three and four o'clock in the morning. Even then we should have to presuppose that they had a motor waiting in some place near at hand. Let us fine that down a little, and say they left the hotel at half-past three at the latest. At this time of the year it is daylight at that hour. Moreover, it is the time of night when the hotel is most quiet.

"There are, to my knowledge, only two exits from the Venetia, one the main exit, which leads to Regent Street. There is—or should have been;—a night-porter on each of those during the night as well as the day. In that case it should not be difficult to discover how many persons if any, passed out during the night, say, between the hours of two and half-past three. And far more easy to find out if those persons carried any luggage with them.

"Guests usually do not leave a hotel at that hour of the night, as the time does not coincide with that of the departure of any trains or boats. So there you are, inspector. Assuming that the dressing-case was dropped in Kent by an aeroplane, you come back to a time of night which makes further investigation easy. And I do not see how you can advance the hour any, as Tinker's evidence that he neither heard nor saw any signs of an aeroplane is most definite, and I think we must accept it."

Inspector Thomas scratched his ear, and gazed at Blake in a contemplative way. He was trying to find out whether Blake had been spoofing him, or whether his deduction, had been meant seriously. At any rate, it certainly provided a lead for investigation which the inspector was determined to follow up without delay. His previous experience of Blake, however, warned him not to commit himself, so he simply grunted:

"There may be something in what you say, and then, again, there may not. All the same, I'll investigate it."

Blake nodded gravely.

"I should, inspector. And, by the way, I presume you would like the dressing-case to take to the Yard as 'Exhibit A'?"

"Well, it really ought to be handed over to the police, you know.

Of course, in your case I shouldn't make a point of it, but—"

Blake laughed outright.

"Which means that you want me to hand it over," he said. "All right, inspector; take it, by all means. I have quite finished with it."

Inspector Thomas glanced suspiciously at Blake; but, nevertheless, he took up the case, and, remarking that he would return later, he took his departure. When, he had gone Williams glanced at Blake.

"Is that what you think, Mr. Blake—that the thieves left the hotel between two and three this morning, and made their escape to the Continent by aeroplane?"

"I shouldn't like to commit myself to anything definite yet," replied Blake; "but I don't mind saying that, personally, I am not inclined at present to consider that theory. It is too soon yet to form any definite skeleton of hypothesis." He turned abruptly to Browning. "I am afraid this business is taking up a good deal of your time, Browning," he said. "But I have got to ask you to lend me your further assistance."

"Why of course, Mr. Blake. Good heavens, this is a terrible thing to happen at the Venetia. If it gets out, it will give us a bad black eye in the business. I have instructions from the management to do everything in my power to assist you to discover the truth."

"Then I am going to ask you for a little information. It would not be difficult for you to let me have a copy of your office list of all the guests staying in the hotel?'

"No. I can give you one in half an hour."

"Good. With that list I should like a little note made opposite each name, stating on what date the guest arrived. Further, I should like a special list of all guests who came yesterday. As far as my memory serves me, the Bretonic was the only mail steamer which arrived yesterday from America. In that case, with the exception of those who came from the Continent, it is fairly safe to assume that most of your guests who arrived about ten o'clock last night from Paddington came by the boat special from Plymouth.

"If we can separate that list from the larger one, then we can easily identify each person as a passenger by the Bretonic by the simple process of having Cunningham, your house detective, go through their rooms quietly and find out how many of them have the Bretonic labels on their luggage. Then again, some of them may have telegraphed for rooms. That would be an additional confirmation of what we are seeking."

"I can find that out easily enough," responded Browning.

"Mrs. Courtlandt sent a wireless from the Bretonic for rooms," volunteered Williams.

"There may have been others," remarked Blake. "After that, Browning, I should like to have a look at the floor plan of the hotel. I want to see the exact arrangement of the rooms on the second and third floors.

CHAPTER 5.   Detailing the Famous Detective's Careful Investigations—His Suspicions—And His Orders to His Assistant.

BROWNING went off at once to arrange for the production of the lists Blake had asked for. He returned a few minutes later to say that the matter had been put in hand, and that the lists would be brought to him just as soon as they had been completed. With him he brought a piece of paper which he spread out on the desk. "I have already got the names of those who reserved rooms by wireless from the Bretonic, or by telegram from Plymouth. There were seven messages altogether—four from the Bretonic and three from Plymouth. They are as follows: From the Bretonic: Mrs. Courtlandt, Mr. Joseph Devra, Mr. Simeon Ferguson, and Miss Nora Biddle. From Plymouth: Mr. and Mrs. Stevenson (I have counted them as one), Sir William Frost and Mr. Arnold Wright."

"Beyond Mrs. Courtlandt, how many of those persons are known to you—if any?" asked Blake.

"Let me see. I don't know Mr. Devra, but I have seen Mr. Ferguson about the hotel at different times. I rather think he lives in London, but he must have been in America, because he wirelessed from the Bretonic. I do not know Miss Biddle, but she came into my office this morning to ask for some information about her letter of credit. She said, in the course of conversation, that she had come to Europe to spend the summer. I do not know Mr. and Mrs. Stevenson, but I know Sir William Frost well, and also Mr. Arnold Wright. The latter is a well known New York journalist who always stays here when he comes to London. That is all, I think."

"I know of Mr. Devra," put in Williams. "He is a dealer in pictures and antiques in New York —a man of unquestioned standing."

"That all helps," remarked Blake. "We have to start with seven guests whom we know came by the Bretonic. All these sent messages, either by wireless or by ordinary telegram, for rooms. Of the number we can, for the time being anyway, eliminate the following: Mr. Devra, Miss Biddle, Sir William Frost—whom I know myself —and Mr. Arnold Wright. I also know of both Mr. Devra and Mr. Wright. Mr. and Mrs. Stevenson we shall make further inquiries about. As for Mr. Simeon Ferguson. I fancy I know a little about him, too. If I am right in my recollection, he is a company promoter of sorts in the

44

City. But we can easily ascertain that. Ah! here is your clerk, Browning. Perhaps he has the list we want."

The manager took from the clerk who had just entered two sheets of paper, and, after a glance at them, said:

"This is the full list of all the guests who came to the hotel yesterday, and another list of those the reception clerk thinks came by the Bretonic. We can confirm that as soon as Cunningham brings his report, he is working through the different rooms now."

Blake took the first list and ran his eye rapidly down it. There were nearly fifty names by count a few of which he knew. Those who had registered with an English address had been written in, with no comment by the clerk, except in the case of those whom he knew. Opposite these names he had put a blue-pencilled cross, with the initials "O. C.," which meant "old customer."

Opposite those who had registered from the Continent and other places abroad he had put a red cross, and likewise the letters "O. C." beside any whom he knew as regular visitors. An additional "A" in some cases told Blake that these represented Americans travelling in Europe who had come from different points in Europe.

The list, including those whom the clerk thought had all arrived by the Bretonic was a separate sheet, and made a total of nineteen names, including the seven they had already dealt with. Of the balance of twelve, three were married couples which Blake marked for further investigation, and two were New York financiers whom he knew by repute.

Williams was able to identify several more names, and remembered seeing some of the others on board. Blake managed to reduce the list little by little, until he had marked for brief inquiry half a dozen names or so, and for detailed inquiry about five more. Then he handed the lists back to Browning.

"There you are," he said. "If you will find out all you can about these people, it will help to narrow things down. But I want to go over the plan of the hotel first."

Just as he spoke a clerk entered with the plan for which Browning had sent. The manager spread it out on his desk and Blake bent over it.

"Now then," he said, "show me just where Mrs. Courtlandt's rooms are."

"Just here," and the manager pointed at a suite.

Blake studied the position of the room for a few minutes. "This along here, I see, is the staircase," and he pointed to a series of parallel lines on the right of the plan.

"Yes that is the main staircase. This one here, on the left of the plan, is the one which serves the east wing."

"I see that between the main staircase and Mrs. Courtlandt's suite there are only three rooms. What are these marks?"

"That is the plan which is used daily, to show exactly what rooms are occupied and what rooms are free. It is shown to visitors if they wish to consult it before choosing their room. The marks to which you refer show that the rooms are already occupied for that day. You will thus see that the first room on the right, after passing the main staircase—this square here represents the lift—was occupied last night. The next room on that side of the corridor was vacant. The next one was occupied, and next comes Mrs. Courtlandt's suite. Beyond her apartments is another suite which was occupied, and then again come single rooms. On the other side of the corridor you will see by the marks that all the rooms were occupied. There are no suites on that side, but you will see by the plan that there are some bedrooms with bathrooms attached."

"I see. I shall want the names of all the occupants of those rooms. Now, then, I take it this is the floor beneath? Well, we won't worry about that at present. This will be the floor above?"

"Yes."

"I notice by the marks that there are three bedrooms on this floor, which correspond to the rooms composing Mrs. Courtlandt's suite."

"That is a slight error in the plan. There are really only two bedrooms; the third is a bathroom, and is directly over the bathroom attached to Mrs. Courtlandt's apartment."

"The bedroom was occupied last night, but the room with the bath was not—at least, I judge so from the marks."

"Yes, that would be so."

"I think that is the room I had," put in Williams, pointing to the plan and indicating the bedroom which was just above Mrs. Courtlandt's sitting-room.

Blake glanced up quickly. "Are you sure?"

"Well, I know I was just above her rooms. Is the number there?"

"Yes—331."

"Then I am right. That is the number of my room."

"Then you must have been directly overhead when the robbery occurred."

"It sure looks that way."

"What time did you retire?"

"About half past eleven. We got here about ten o'clock. I hung about for a while to see if Mrs. Courtlandt wanted me for anything. Then I had supper, smoked a cigar in the lounge, and went upstairs."

"Are you a sound sleeper?"

"Not particularly, and I wake very easily. I might have slept a little more soundly than usual last night, as I was very tired."

"Yet you heard or saw nothing of a suspicious nature?"

"Absolutely nothing."

Blake was about to ask another question, when the door opened and Inspector Thomas reappeared. A single glance at his face told Blake that his sleuthing had been barren of results.

"Nothing doing," he announced curtly. "I followed up that theory of yours, Mr. Blake, but there is nothing in it. There was a porter on duty at both doors all night, and two clerks on duty in the main office, not counting the assistant cashier. Only one or two late guests came into the hotel around that time, and no one went out. If anyone had, they would have been certain to see them."

"Then, what about your aeroplane, inspector?" asked Blake, with a smile.

"I don't believe you thought the escape was worked that way," remarked the inspector suspiciously.

"It was you who said so, not I," responded Blake. "Personally, I did not think so, and do not think so, inspector."

"Then what do you think?" asked the other irascibly. "I must confess it's one of the queerest cases I have ever been up against."

"I agree with you on that point. But I am as much in the dark as you. You have the dressing-case; you have heard all Tinker can tell you about it. It's up to you, inspector."

"Well, I am going on to the Yard to think things over," grunted Inspector Thomas. "Will you keep in touch with me? I have just seen Mrs. Courtlandt. She was going out. She asked me not to allow anything to become public yet, and she is offering a private reward of ten thousand pounds for the recovery of the jewels."

"Very handsome, indeed," agreed Blake. "I hope you succeed in landing it, inspector."

If the inspector had gained anything further of value he kept it to himself, and departed for the Yard. Shortly after Cunningham, the house detective, returned with his report. His surreptitious examination of the luggage in the different rooms which he had visited confirmed the list of the reception-clerk without exception. Thus Blake now had a full list of names on which to work. These lists he handed over to Tinker.

"Take these, Tinker, and go with Cunningham. Get every scrap of information you can. If I have left the hotel, bring your report on to Baker Street. If I am still here, we will go over it in Mr. Browning's office. I think it would be as well for you to go with them, Mr. Williams. You may be able to tell my assistant a good deal about different American guests. And don't forget, Tinker, I want you to confine your attention particularly to those who arrived by the Bretonic."

When the three had departed, Blake turned to Browning. "That begins to get the decks cleared for action," he said. "Now the next thing I want to do is to make an examination of the two rooms above Mrs. Courtlandt's— I mean Williams' room, as well as the one that was unoccupied last night."

Browning knew Blake too well to show any surprise at his request. He rose at once. "I will come along with you," was all he said.

Leaving the office they went along the narrow corridor which led to the reception desk and the lobby. As they turned into the lobby Blake made a quick movement, as though he intended turning back, then he recovered himself quickly and went on towards the lift.

But all the way up to the third floor he was thinking: "Now, that was Simeon Ferguson. It is the same man I thought. And that other man was Thurlow Jordan I have seen him knocking about the West End a lot. And I am also positive I saw him dining with Ferguson one night about a month ago. Now, where was it I saw them?"

Blake racked his brains trying to remember, and, just as they reached Williams' room, the recollection came to him. "It was at Bellano's," he muttered to himself. "I knew I had seen them together. They were friendly enough then. Now, why did they just pass each other in the lounge without speaking. They acted like complete strangers. I don't know much about either of them, but I think, all the same, I shall make a few inquiries. If Jordan is staying in the hotel, he will come under the fine-tooth combing that Tinker is giving all the visitors." He turned to Browning. "I noticed Thurlow Jordan in the lobby just now," he said carelessly. "Is he staying here?"

"Yes. He came back yesterday afternoon."

Blake filed the fact for future reference, and gave all his attention to his examination of Williams' room. Not that he had any suspicions of the New York detective, who had been detailed to keep watch and ward over Mrs. Stuyvesant Courtlandt and her jewels. As far as he knew, Williams was perfectly straight, and his attitude had been quite frank in every way. At the same time, a certain germ of an idea was working in Blake's mind, and, in order to cultivate it, so to say, it was necessary for him to make a detailed examination of the rooms over those occupied by Mrs. Courtlandt.

Inspector Thomas would have been puzzled could he have known that the investigations Blake was making, at that moment, had been inspired by nothing less than the dressing-case which, at the same time, he was studying at Scotland Yard.

Blake ignored the detective's luggage, and confined himself to a very careful examination of the floor and the windows. He did not anticipate being disturbed by the occupant of the room, as he knew the work Tinker was engaged on would keep them busy for a considerable time.

His suggestion that Williams should accompany the lad had, as its prime motive, his desire to be alone during his present examination. He spent about half-an-hour in the room while Browning, who could make neither head nor tail of Blake's procedure, looked on. When Blake had finished, he said:

"Now for the next room, Browning. I needn't say that I don't want Williams to know that I have taken the liberty of entering his room."

"I quite understand. Shall we go to the next room now?"

"Please."

Browning led the way and opened the door with his master-key. It was a large bedroom, and, on the left, was a door half-open, through which Blake could see a bathroom. The two rooms coincided exactly to the bedroom and bathroom of the suite beneath, while the box-room they had just left was, of course, exactly above the sitting-room occupied by Mrs. Courtlandt.

Blake made a tour of the room, casting his eyes this way and that, until he came to the window on the right—there were two. He lifted the lower sash, and, leaning out, gazed upwards and downwards. The view of the inner court of the hotel was similar to that from the floor below. Then, taking out his pocket magnifying glass, he began to make a detailed examination of the window-sill and the iron grille outside. It was slow, tedious work, and Browning was obviously bored, for, after some time, he said: "If you don't mind I will go down to my office and see if there is anything to be attended to. I shall be back presently."

Blake nodded absently and went on with his work. Not a single particle of the surface of either the grille or the window-sill escaped his keen eye. This part of his work completed, he dropped to his knees and began to make a similar study of the floor beneath the window.

As he always did in this type of examination, he blocked out the area to be scutinised into a number of imaginary squares, each of which he brought within the focus of the magnifying glass. Nor did he leave a square until he had exhausted every tiny bit of the area. In this way he moved back and forth, pausing now and then for a longer time than usual. Twice he took a pair of thin tweezers from his pocket and, picking up something with the greatest care, deposited it inside a thin specimen wallet which he took from an inner pocket.

When he had exhausted the area by the first window, he moved on to the part of the carpet beneath the second, he repeated his actions there, and had covered about half the area he had blocked out, when, suddenly, he bent swiftly and with the tweezers again picked up something. It was considerably more easy of examination by the naked eye than the other two specimens he had gathered, and, before depositing it in the wallet, he held it to the light for a few minutes.

As he put it away a peculiar gleam came into his eye. Tinker would have known that that gleam meant Blake had formed a theory of some sort, and that he had found something which tended to confirm his theory. It might be one dealing with only a very small phase of the case, or one covering what he thought would prove to be the main avenue of investigation. As a matter of fact, in the present instance, the former was the case. He had been looking for a certain thing and he had found it, although, when he had started out, he had had no idea whether he would find it in some room on the third floor or on the second floor—even if he found it at all.

Once more he rescued something from the floor with the thin

tweezers, but nothing else of any interest was revealed over the balance of the area. Getting to his feet Blake raised the sash of the second window and continued his examination there.

He repeated his former procedure at the first window, with the exception that his study of the upper surface of the top bar of the iron grille consumed considerably more time. He was engaged in a scrutiny of the under surface when Browning returned. As he entered the room Blake straightened up. "I have just finished," he announced.

"Find anything?"

"Not much, I am afraid. Do you know how Tinker is getting on?"

"They are nearly finished I believe."

Blake nodded. "I can do no more until I get the particulars he is after. I particularly want the list of names of all those who occupied rooms on this floor, and the floor beneath, in this wing. With that and the other lists you have secured, I shall be in a better position to proceed. By the way, I want to have a talk to the reception-clerk who was on duty yesterday afternoon and evening. What time does he come on duty?"

"At twelve o'clock."

Blake glanced at his watch. "It is twenty minutes to twelve now. I will see him before I leave the hotel. The man on duty now is the one, I presume, who was at the desk yesterday morning."

"Yes."

"I want to have a talk to him as well. I will do so while I am waiting for Tinker. That finishes here for the present, Browning. You might see Mrs. Courtlandt when she returns, and tell her that I am working on the case and hope to have some news for her soon. You might add that it is necessary for her to continue, for the present, as if nothing had happened. If this business gets out and the papers feature it, which they are bound to do in a robbery of such magnitude, then our work will be much more difficult."

They returned to the ground floor where Blake parted from Browning. He approached the reception desk and asked the clerk in charge if he could spare him a moment in private. They went along to a small room adjoining Browning's office, where Blake began to question the reception-clerk.

"I have been studying the floor plan of the hotel," he said. "I gather from Mr. Browning that the plan is prepared daily, and shows what rooms are occupied and what are free."

"Yes, it is prepared each morning. It saves a good deal of time, for the man on duty can see at a glance what rooms he can give to a new arrival, and also, in the case of fussy guests, it can be seen by the plan just where the room is situated. That saves showing over several rooms."

"I see. But I don't suppose it is very generally consulted by visitors, is it?"

"Oh, no. As a matter of fact, we use it for that purpose very rarely. Most of our visitors accept a room from our description of it."

"That is what I thought. It would be unusual, then, for a guest arriving, to insist upon an examination of the plan?"

"Yes, quite."

"Do you recall any such incident yesterday."

"Not at the moment. I could ask the other clerk, who relieves me at twelve."

"No, don't trouble, please. I shall do that. You know, of course, that I am making a private investigation for the management."

"Yes."

"Can you recall anything—no matter how trivial—which happened yesterday while you were on duty, that you could possibly connect with Mrs. Stuyvesant Courtlandt?"

The reception-clerk thought hard for a few minutes. "Well I can't say I do," he replied finally. "Yesterday morning a messenger-boy brought a letter for her. I told him that she had not arrived, but he said his orders were to leave it. That is all. I just put it in the box under her room number until she arrived."

"Thank you. I will go back to the office with you. I want to have a word with your relief."

On reaching the lobby Blake found that the relief man had just come on. He repeated his inquiries in exactly the same way and, when he had finished, he had gathered just one more fact which he tucked away mentally for reference. He had barely finished when Browning brought him the new list for which he had asked, showing the names of each guest who occupied a room on the second and third floors, in the same wing where Mrs. Courtlandt's suite was situated. Blake thrust this into his pocket and returned to the lobby. He saw Tinker coming towards him with Cunningham and Williams.

"We have just finished, guv'nor," announced the lad.

"Good, then we shall go on to Baker Street at once. I have a little work to do there."

"Have you discovered anything?" asked Williams anxiously.

"Not yet. I shall return to the hotel some time during the afternoon, Mr. Williams. In the meantime, you can be of assistance if you will join Mr. Cunningham and dig up any more facts you think will be of use to us."

With that he and Tinker took their departure. They had just reached the front courtyard, and were waiting for a taxi, when Blake suddenly touched Tinker on the arm.

"That taxi, my lad," he said in a low tone. "Go after it—see where it goes and report as soon as possible at Baker Street. If I am not there you will find a note on the desk saying where I have gone. Off with you."

Tinker slipped into the taxi which had been called for him and Blake, and drove off after the one which had just turned into Piccadilly. In it Blake had recognised Thurlow Jordan, who had roused his curiosity in the lounge about an hour before, and about whom he had been thinking almost exclusively since his interrogation of the relief reception-clerk.

CHAPTER 6.   Blake's Ruse—Tinker Makes Good—What Blake Saw in the Bookshop.

AS soon as Tinker had disappeared in the wake of Thurlow Jordan, Blake secured another taxi. Instead of driving direct to Baker Street as he had intended, he instructed the man to go on to Scotland Yard. There he made his way up to the plainly-furnished room occupied by Inspector Thomas.

He found the inspector seated at his desk, in the act of making a very detailed examination of the dressing-case which Blake had handed over. He set it on the floor and looked at Blake inquiringly. Blake bent down, and, picking up the case, held up the end of the green cord which had been tied round the handle.

"How do you think that got there, inspector?" he asked.

"Why, I suppose it has had an address label tied to the handle at some time."

"That is what I thought at first. But just as I was about to leave for Baker Street, inspector, an idea came to me. I thought I would pass it on to you."

"What is that, Blake?"

"We know that this case contained Mrs. Courtlandt's jewels."

"Yes."

"It also has her initials on the outside and her name on the inside."

"Yes."

"Well, now, does it seem likely that she would have a label tied to a case which was supposed to be in her personal keeping all the time?"

The inspector pulled his ear, a favourite habit when he was nonplussed. "Hang it that never occurred to me."

"Nor to me, until a little while ago. But it should be easy enough to settle. Mrs. Courtlandt has gone out, but she should be back at the Venetia soon. Why don't you ask her? She would remember whether a label had been tied to the handle or not."

"Haven't you asked her yet?"

"No."

"And you are serious?"

"Perfectly."

"Then I will ask her. I will take the case along and show her the cord."

"A good idea, inspector. Will you telephone me and let me know the result?"

"I certainly shall."

"Right."

Blake replaced the dressing-case on the floor, and, as his hand went casually towards his waistcoat pocket, Inspector Thomas never for a single moment dreamed that between Blake's fingers was a tiny twist of the green cord which he had detached while he had been speaking. As Blake descended to the courtyard he smiled to himself.

"Fair exchange is no robbery," he muttered. "I fancy I have given the inspector a tip that should prove to be quite as valuable as the little twist of cord I took—if he follows it up in the right way."

Back at Baker Street, Blake seated himself at the desk in the consulting room and picked up the file containing the morning papers. He turned to those of the preceding day, and made a careful study of the weather reports and forecasts. Then he slipped the file into its rack and, rising, walked across to where a large map of the British Isles hung on the wall.

With his pencil he traced out a faint line beginning at London and following a course that had been suggested to him by what he had read in the weather reports. At last the point of his pencil came to rest at a spot in Kent.

"It certainly proves out," he muttered. "The wind last night was forecasted as being light, from ten to twelve miles an hour, and the direction from W. by N. Well, that direction and that velocity would convey a drifting object in about four hours to somewhere near this spot where the tip of my pencil rests. And this is roughly the location of Lord Ranborough's country place in Kent. If one follows up that suggestion and works back from the time Tinker found the dressing-case in the plantation, then four hours or so earlier would bring it back to somewhere round two o'clock in the morning in London. Hm! Now I wonder if that theory will stand the acid test. I'll try it at any rate."

With that Blake turned, and, opening the door into the side corridor, made his way along to the laboratory. There he busied himself for some minutes arranging the powerful microscope which formed such an important adjunct to so many of Blake's investigations. When it had been adjusted to his satisfaction he turned on the powerful lateral light and seated himself.

First he took from his pocket the wisp of green cord which he had abstracted surreptitiously while in Inspector Thomas' office. This he laid very carefully on a tiny glass slide. Next, he took out the small wallet, in which he had placed the minute specimens he had collected in the bedroom at the Venetia, which adjoined that occupied by the American sleuth. With the aid of a pair of tweezers he placed these carefully beside the other; then he thrust the slide under the magnifying lens.

For some minutes Blake studied the specimens through the tube, turning them over occasionally with the tweezers. When he had finished, he gathered them all up and replaced them in the specimen wallet. That done, he turned out the lateral light and replaced the microscope in its case.

"Whatever the truth may be," he murmured, as he made his way back to the consulting room, "one thing is certainly a fact—the wisp of green cord which I got from the piece that was tied round the handle of the dressing-case, and those tiny particles I picked up in the room at the Venetia are undoubtedly identical. If they did not come from the same length of cord, I am prepared to state categorically they were at least made in the same factory and of the same spinning. But that does not explain how I can link up that connection."

Just as Blake re-entered the consulting room the telephone rang. Lifting the receiver he found that it was Inspector Thomas speaking from Browning's private room at the Venetia.

"I made that inquiry, Blake," he said. "You certainly thought of a good point there, but I don't see what it will lead to."

"Just what do you mean, inspector?"

"Well, Mrs. Courtlandt is quite positive that she never saw the green cord before, and equally emphatic in saying that it was not tied on the handle when she retired last night. Williams and the maid say the same. Mrs. Courtlandt wants to know where we found the case, but I didn't tell her."

"Nor should I, yet," responded Blake. "It seems to me, inspector, that this has raised a point worth looking into. Find who tied that cord round the handle, and you will be hot on the trail of the person, or persons, who had the dressing-case in their possession last night." And without giving the inspector a chance to ask him what he meant, Blake hung up the receiver.

He was busily writing down the notes of his investigations so far, when the door opened and Tinker came in.

"Well, I followed him all right, guv'nor," he announced. "After leaving the Venetia the taxi drove to Old Compton Street, Soho. It stopped before an old book shop. Our man got out and went into the shop. I drove on a little way and watched. He was in the place about half-an-hour. When he came out he drove back to the Venetia. I followed him that far and came back here to report."

"A book shop in Soho," muttered Blake. "Do you know if he made a purchase there, Tinker?"

"I don't think so, guv'nor. Anyway, he wasn't carrying any parcel with him when he came out. The only thing I noticed was that when he went into the shop he was wearing a light overcoat, and when he came out he carried it over his arm."

"I remember seeing the coat on him when he left the hotel," said Blake. "So he had apparently taken it off in the shop, had he?"

"Yes."

"All right, my lad. Now, I have another job for you. Listen carefully to what I say. I want you to return to the Venetia. Scout around the hotel until you get a line on Thurlow Jordan and Simeon Ferguson. There is one point in particular that I want to discover, if possible. Some time ago I saw Jordan and Ferguson dining together in a Jermyn Street restaurant. But this morning I saw them pass each other in the lobby of the Venetia without speaking to each other. I want, if possible, to find out if that was intentional or accidental—whether a pose or whether the two men have perhaps had some disagreement. Do you understand?"

"Yes, guv'nor."

"They may be lunching as it is now lunch time, or they may be in the bar, or in the lounge, Anyway, try and find them. Before you do that, however, there is something I want you to attempt first. Kelly, the door man, may be of some use to you."

"What is that, guv'nor?"

"I will show you."

As he spoke, Blake took the specimen wallet from his pocket and with a pair of tweezers took out the tiny fragments of cord which he had examined under the microscope. Next he took up a powerful magnifying glass and motioned for the lad to make an examination. When he had done so Tinker glanced up inquiringly.

"What's the idea, guv'nor?"

"This. I want you to get hold of the floor valet who looks after the rooms occupied by Jordan and Ferguson. He should know what clothes they wore last evening. It might be a good idea to get Cunningham to arrange it for you. Personally, I fancy you will find they both dressed before dinner.

"Through the valet get the pair of trousers each man wore. In all probability he has already brushed and folded them away, but we will hope that in this instance the valeting was perfunctory. It usually is under hotel conditions. Take the trousers, and go over the legs very carefully with this glass. I want you to pay particular attention to the knees. What you are to look for is any signs of bits of fluff. If you see any, collect the bits with the blade of your knife and bring them back here. Is that clear?"

"Perfectly."

"Very well. Needless to say, have the trousers replaced immediately you have finished your examination, and, through Cunningham, arrange that the floor valet shall say nothing to either Jordan or Ferguson."

"All right, guv'nor."

With that, Tinker slipped the magnifying glass in his pocket and left the room. When he was gone Blake worked away at his notes for some time, then, when he had finished, he drew the telephone instrument towards him. He got through to a number at Croydon, and, had anybody been listening, they would have been extremely puzzled at Blake's conversation with the person at the other end of the wire.

That individual happened to be the meteorological expert of one of the big cross-Channel flying companies, and apparently Blake's talk was of a satisfactory nature, for, as he hung up the receiver, he was smiling queerly.

Then Blake did an even more puzzling thing for one who was supposed to be devoting every thought to the unravelling of the robbery of the Courtlandt gems. First he stuffed his old pipe, and, crossing to the leaded glass bookcases which stood against the opposite wall, took out several numbers of a certain highly technical scientific journal. He examined the contents tables of one after the other, until he seemed to find what he sought.

Replacing the others in the case, he dropped into a saddle-bag chair and turned to the article for which he had been looking. That he had read it before was evident from the pencilled annotations, some of assent, some of dissent, which he had made in the margins of the pages.

The article was entitled: "Some Suggestions as to the Probable Development of Aeronautical Science in its Relation to Future Warfare," and the author of the very abstruse paper was one Professor Andrew Butterfield.

It was the type of thing that might be read and appreciated by a few scientists and specialists in various professions during the quiet hours of the night, but it was certainly not the type of thing upon which one would expect even Blake to regale himself just before lunch.

But that he found it exceedingly absorbing was plain, for he read each word with the utmost attention, and scarcely heard the sound of the door as Tinker re-entered the consulting-room. Blake looked up with a frown as his attention was drawn from the paper.

"You are back soon," he said.

Tinker looked surprised.

"Not so soon, guv'nor. It is more than an hour since I left."

It was Blake's turn to show surprise.

"I had no idea it was so late. Well, what luck, my lad?"

"I don't know yet, guv'nor; but I did what you told me to do. I got hold of Cunningham, and he managed to get the trousers that Jordan and Ferguson wore last night. We took them to Cunningham's room, where I examined them through the glass. I didn't find anything on Jordan's; but there was a little bit of fluff on the right knee of Ferguson's pair. I scraped it off carefully, and have brought it with me. Cunningham was no end keen to know what the game was."

"And then?"

"After that I scouted about looking for Jordan and Ferguson. I saw Jordan in the grillroom and Ferguson was in the bar. He came out just as I got there, and I went after him. When he made for the courtyard and I saw Kelly signal for a taxi, I thought I would follow him just to see where he went."

"Not a bad idea, Tinker. What happened?"

"You will be surprised when I tell you, guv'nor. He drove to the very same bookshop in Soho where Jordan went this morning."

"Ah!" Blake's voice was sharp with satisfaction. "You did better work there than you thought, my lad."

"How do you mean, guv'nor?"

"I can't tell you, yet, because there are too many loose ends still to be picked up. One of them we may find through an examination of the fluff you have brought. Come along to the laboratory. We will put it under the microscope."

When Blake had turned on the lateral light of the powerful instrument he took the folded piece of paper which Tinker handed him, and, with a fine pair of tweezers, placed the tiny ball of fluff on a glass slide.

Thrusting the slide very carefully under the tube, he applied his eye to the eyepiece, and for some minutes there was dead silence while he studied what now appeared as a mountainous mass of tangled wool. Presently he lifted his head and took out his specimen wallet. From it he took his own specimens and laid them on the slide a little distance from the other ball.

Then he again bent to his examination. He spent nearly ten minutes this time, occasionally moving the little piles slightly with the thin tweezers. When he finally lifted his head he turned to Tinker.

"Take a look, my lad. I may want you to confirm my evidence, one day."

Tinker did as he was bid, while Blake jotted down a few notes. When the lad looked up, he said:

"There isn't much to be seen, guv'nor, except a tangle of threads."

"Quite so. What colour seems to predominate in the specimens which came from my wallet."

"Green," replied Tinker promptly.

"Exactly. Now look again, and tell me what you can make of the little ball of fluff which you collected."

Tinker obeyed, and soon, with his eye still at the eyepiece, he said:

"I can see some bits of green of the same colour as the threads in your pile, guv'nor. I can also see some red, some purple and some black."

"Good, that exactly confirms my own examination. Now we will collect the specimens very carefully, keeping them separate. For your own information, Tinker, I will say that the bits of green in your pile are, in my opinion, tiny shreds from the same piece from which my specimens originally came. The red and purple I take to be minute bits of fluff from the carpet upon which the man who wore those trousers knelt. The black, I fancy, will be from the trousers, themselves, some of the material which came away as you scraped the surface with your knife."

"Yes, guv'nor, but I don't see what you are getting at," protested Tinker.

"Keep your ears and eyes open and you will soon discover," responded Blake, as he placed the specimens very carefully in the wallet and switched out the lateral light. "Now come along to lunch. I have further work for you to do this afternoon."

A good deal mystified, Tinker followed his master to the dining-room, where Mrs. Bardell had just laid lunch. During the meal the lad was considerably bored as Blake insisted on carrying on a conversation dealing with highly technical researches, which, it appeared, some foreign governments were making in aeronautical science—a conversation which at last developed into a monologue on Blake's part, for, although Tinker was keen enough on flying and the various means of adapting the science to warfare, it was from the strictly elemental point of view of waggling the joy-stick between his knees.

And never for a single moment did the lad dream that the boring dissertation, to which he was forced to listen, had a direct bearing on the case on which they were then working.

Blake's eyes were twinkling a little as he rose from the table, but he took no pains to enlighten Tinker. Instead, he said:

"I want you to return to the Venetia this afternoon, my lad. You may, or may not, find either Jordan, or Ferguson, or both there. If you do, just keep your eyes open, and, if one of them leaves the hotel, follow him. I, myself, am going along to investigate that bookshop in Soho. Oh, and by the way, see Browning as soon as you reach the Venetia. Arrange with him to have the tip passed along to us, at once, if either Jordan or Ferguson give up their rooms."

When Tinker had departed Blake smoked a cigar; then he went along to his dressing-room. It was a very different looking person who emerged half an hour later. No longer was it the well-dressed Sexton Blake, but a distinctly shabby-looking person, whose long, unkempt hair and thick lensed spectacles gave the impression of a very out-at-heels individual of, perhaps, literary or artistic leanings.

Under his arm he carried a couple of old books. Blake walked as far as Oxford Street where he caught a 'bus for Piccadilly Circus. There he dismounted and walked slowly along Shaftesbury Avenue until he came to a narrow street that led into Soho.

He strolled leisurely along to Old Compton Street, and, along that thoroughfare, until he saw the second-hand bookshop, the address of which Tinker had given him.

He stood outside for some time examining the ragged array of books there; then he entered the shop. It was a gloomy place, piled in extraordinary confusion with hundreds upon hundreds of old books and journals. No attempt seemed ever to have been made at cataloguing or classification, and it was evident that sales were only made of books picked out personally by the would-be purchaser.

At the moment of his entrance, Blake saw two or three people engrossed in making a selection from the chaotic piles of volumes. Behind the counter, and almost hidden from view, was a thin, Jewish-looking young man whose features seemed more suited to the surroundings of a pawn shop. He did not glance up until Blake laid his two books on the counter.

"Will you buy these?" asked Blake.

The young man surveyed him briefly, then picked up the books. One of them he tossed aside almost at once, with the words: "One and six for that." Over the other he spent a longer time. As a matter of fact, it was an early edition of Moliere which Blake had picked up in Paris, and which he knew to be quite genuine.

A duplicate had come into his hands later, and he didn't mind parting with one of them. When the young man glanced up and said: "I don't mind making you an offer for this—say thirty shillings," Blake smiled.

"It is quiet genuine," he said. "I was counting on getting six pounds."

"Nothing doing here," snapped the youth. "I don't say it ain't genuine, but books are a drag at the present time. I might go to two pounds more—no more."

Blake reduced his demands to five, and, after some haggling, the clerk raised his bid to two pounds ten. Blake was in no hurry, and was quite prepared to continue the haggling as long as the other would raise his bid.

He managed to stretch it out for nearly half an hour, then he finally accepted three pounds six shillings, on the understanding that he was to make purchases in the shop to the extent of at least two pounds. This suited Blake exactly, so after the transaction was completed he took up his money and turned to the shelves behind him.

It was now getting on for four o'clock, and as Blake was prepared to put in a good two hours if necessary, he went about his choosing very leisurely. The young man had returned to the journal which had absorbed his attention, and the other occupants of the shop were still engrossed in their reading.

Up to now Blake had not the faintest idea what loose thread he might come upon in the second-hand bookshop. His visit there had been solely inspired by Tinker's report. There was nothing remarkable in the fact that Thurlow Jordan had visited the shop during the forenoon.

It was not exactly the type of place in which one would expect a man like Jordan to be interested, but there could be half a dozen simple explanations for the reason of his visit. But when Tinker had returned to Baker Street, with the information that Simeon Ferguson had also gone to the same place, the coincidence struck Blake as a little too pointed to be ignored.

Had it not been for that little incident he had seen in the lobby of the Venetia, he would not have been so quick to attach any importance to the movements of the two persons in question. Like several other individuals, their names were on the list of those arrivals at the hotel whose credentials had been under examination, and which had been narrowed down, to just a few.

Among that few had been both Jordan and Ferguson, but, so far, Blake had nothing of a very definite nature to go upon. True, Tinker's work at the hotel had placed one loose end in Blake's hands, but that was altogether too circumstantial to be of any real value.

At the same time, he was distinctly suspicious of the pair, although he had to confess that there was one very strong element in the case that made it seem very difficult to connect them with the disappearance of Mrs. Courtlandt's jewels, and the finding of her dressing-case forty miles from London, early in the morning, following the theft.

There was another germ of suggestion working in Blake's brain, and it was to try and pick up a thread that would turn that suggestion into a definite lead, that he had visited the bookshop.

So far he had seen absolutely nothing which opened up any lane of suggestion. The place was obviously a perfectly genuine shop, devoted to the purchase and sale of second-hand books. The young man behind the counter might appear more suited to a pawnshop, but that he knew his business had been proven by Blake when he had appraised the Moliere edition.

Under the present trade depression, Blake knew that he would probably not have received any more for the volume at any other dealers. And yet, why was it that two men whom he had seen dining together one evening many weeks ago, who were both staying at the Venetia, but who now appeared not to be acquainted, should have chosen to visit this little out of the way second-hand bookshop on the same day? It was the answer to that puzzle that he was seeking.

Blake's mind was far more busy mulling over this problem than in making any real attempt to choose books, to the value which had been a necessary condition of the sale of the Moliere volume. At the same time he went through the methodical movements of examination, and, in the space of half an hour, had selected two which came to a total value of fourteen shillings.

That left him twenty-six shillings to make up so he moved along a pile of shelves at the rear of the establishment. Here he was quite out of sight of the other occupants of the shop. He saw between the tiers, a door which he concluded must lead to premises at the back. Probably living-rooms, he concluded as he took down a volume. Opening it, he saw that it was an old book of Canadian history, and he settled down to read.

He was so engaged when suddenly the sound of voices reached him from beyond the door near which he stood. They were only a low mumble, and he could not distinguish what was being said. But a few seconds later, they drew nearer, and Blake stepped a little to one side.

Then the door was pulled open and over the top of his book Blake saw a man emerge. He was short, and fat, and obviously a Jew. He was in his shirt sleeves and was smoking a black cigar. Blake decided swiftly that he must be the father of the youth behind the counter, for the younger man reproduced in exact degree the hooked nose of the elder.

But it was the person who then emerged at the heels of the Jew who engaged Blake's keen attention—so keen that he sank his head well below the level of the book. For the man who then came out was none other than Dr. Huxton Rymer.

He brushed past Blake with a brief glance at the shabby person who seemed to be engrossed in a volume of dry history. From the corner of his eye, Blake saw that Rymer carried a large volume, and that it was supposed to be the reason for his interview in the Jew's private sanctum was evident, for, as they reached the middle of the shop Blake heard the Jew say:

"Tham, wrap up thith book for Professor Butterfield. He hath dethided to take it."

Professor Butterfield! The name fell on Blake's ears with a shock. Professor Butterfield! There was only one Professor Butterfield of whom Blake had ever heard, and that was the erudite scientist who had been writing such abstruse papers to the scientific journals during the past few mouths. Professor Butterfield! And yet Blake was absolutely certain that the man who had just passed him was none other than Dr. Huxton Rymer.

Sexton Blake closed his book of Canadian history and swiftly noted the price which had been scribbled in pencil on the fly leaf. Nine shillings. Rapidly he made the calculation. He must choose further books to the value of seventeen shillings to make up the two pounds. Above him was a volume marked ten shellings. Blake drew it from the shelf, the while his eye ran swiftly over the other volumes. At last he found what he wanted a book with a price tag of seven shillings. It was a bulky volume relating to chicken breeding, but that didn't matter to Blake. With his two pounds worth of books he approached the counter, just as Professor Butterfield passed out to the street. Blake showed the volumes to the young Jew, who passed them with a nod; the next moment the shabby-looking man, who was Sexton Blake, emerged into Old Compton Street in time to see his quarry disappear round the corner, apparently heading for Shaftesbury Avenue.

CHAPTER 7. Blake Makes an Interesting Discovery—A Curious Experiment—What the Diamond Broker Had to Say.

BLAKE'S surmise was correct, for, as he himself turned the corner, he caught sight of Rymer not far ahead. The latter was walking briskly, apparently quite unaware that he was being followed, Blake quickened his pace a little as his quarry turned into Shaftesbury Avenue, and well it was that he did so, for he was just in time to see Rymer hail a taxi, Blake turned sharply, and searched along the moving traffic until he spotted a cab with the flag up. The driver did not seem particularly keen to take up the shabby-looking fare, but before he had time to argue Blake had thrust a ten-shilling note into his hand.

"That cab ahead," he said curtly. "Go after it. That note is above your fare if you keep it in sight."

The "palm oil" was sufficient for the driver, who gave a nod and started off. It proved to be easy enough to follow the other taxi, for it drove along Shaftesbury Avenue until it reached Piccadilly Circus. There it turned up Piccadilly until it came to Hyde Park Corner, turning there in the direction of Victoria. It drew into the station yard, and as he saw his quarry get out and enter the station Blake followed suit.

He kept well out of sight while Rymer approached the ticket window and purchased a ticket. Then Blake saw him walk along and study the board on which had been chalked the hours of outgoing and incoming trains. From his coign of vantage, Blake tried to make out just which train was interesting Rymer, and, as the latter went along to the buffet Blake thought the one that had interested him had been that which was due to leave for Horsham in about ten minutes.

He decided, in any event, that he would take a chance, so approaching the ticket window he bought a ticket for that place. Then he hung about the news stall until he saw Rymer come out of the buffet, and make for the platform. Blake followed him at a discreet distance and gave a grunt of satisfaction as he saw Rymer enter the Horsham train.

Blake himself entered a carriage near the back of the train, and chose a corner seat from which he could watch the platform. But when, a few minutes later, the train pulled out, he saw that Rymer was still on board.

As the speed increased Blake settled back and lighted a cigarette. He was glad that he had the carriage to himself for a very startling suggestion had obtruded itself into his mind, and he wanted time to mull it over.

"It is certainly a very strange coincidence," he muttered. "In trying to puzzle out just how that empty dressing-case happened to get in the plantation on Ranborough's place, I tried out half a dozen theories. I am quite convinced that it never dropped from any passing aeroplane, although I am strongly of the opinion that those responsible desired to create just that impression in case the article was picked up. It was equally unlikely that it had been thrown into the plantation by someone who had approached the place either by car or on foot. In the first place, the road is a considerable distance away, and, in the second, Tinker is quite certain that it dropped from one of the trees. That seems to point to the probability that it came there from overhead. That was when my mind went back to an article that I had read a short time ago, and in which I had been deeply interested.

"That article dealt with the automatic dropping of explosives over any given area by small drifting balloons, on which the dropping device could be timed in exact ratio with the speed of the wind blowing at the moment of sending up. And that article was written by Professor Andrew Butterfield.

"So far, so good, and it wasn't very difficult to take that theory a step further, and form a tentative hypothesis that this very plan might be employed to drop other objects a considerable distance away from the spot where the miniature balloon was sent up. However, that is a point which, with Stacey's assistance, I hope to clear up to-night. (Stacey was the name of the meteorological expert at Croydon to whom Blake had telephoned earlier in the day.)

"But when I formed that hypothesis, I had no idea that this Professor Butterfield was none other than Dr. Huxton Rymer. That now seems certain, and I must say that it is a very strange coincidence that Rymer should have been visiting the same bookshop to which Tinker tracked both Jordan and Ferguson.

"Now, just what does that mean? What connection can there be, if any, between those visits? What reason had Jordan and Ferguson to go there to-day? And what business has taken Rymer there this afternoon? If one set of coincidences has no relation to the other, then it is a very strange thing that what I discovered at the Venetia should have recalled the article by Professor Butterfield which I had read, and which seemed to me to open up a possible solution of that part of the puzzle.

"Now, is it likely that either Jordan or Ferguson read that article? Neither man seems the type who would indulge in reading of that sort. They would incline more to the sporting papers, if I am any judge. On the other hand, if they have a close connection with the affair at the Venetia, a thing I am beginning to suspect most strongly, then, at what or at whose instigation did they employ that means?

"Where Rymer is then is there some criminal activity is a pretty safe conclusion regarding him, but in view of my warning to him a few months ago, I cannot believe that he has been so foolish as to place himself again in a position in this country where he must be a fugitive from the police. Then what connection, if any, has he with Jordan and Ferguson? And where does the fat Jew at the bookshop come into this? He, of course, might be a fence, and that I can soon ascertain.

"So far, I have been able to reconstruct a little of what must have happened last night. Firstly, I am convinced that the robbery was an 'inside' job designed by no ordinary mind. Every detail was most carefully planned, and there is scarcely a loose end to pick up. It was carried out with daring and precision—absolutely according to plan.

"I am inclined to think the trap was laid before Mrs. Courtlandt arrived at the Venetia, and that the whole success or failure of the plot depended on whether she gave the dressing-case into the safe keeping of the hotel cashier, or took it to her own room for the night. That she did so made the plan possible of execution. Had she not done so, I feel sure the attempt would have failed, or, more likely, it would never have been made. Then what have we? The robbery must have taken place something between midnight and two o'clock in the morning.

"If my hypothesis is correct, then that dressing-case was still in the hotel about that time. But about four hours later, it is picked up forty miles away in a small isolated plantation in Kent. And again, if I am on the right line, then those who perpetrated the robbery were still in the hotel this morning when it was discovered, or, at least, in the neighbourhood of eight o'clock, anyway.

"It is there that there seems to be a direct connection between the piece of green cord which was tied round the handle of the dressing-case, the bits I picked up in the vacant room, which was directly above Mrs. Courtlandt's bedroom, and the wisps that Tinker managed to collect from the knee of the trousers that Ferguson wore last night.

"That undoubtedly brings Ferguson directly under suspicion, and notwithstanding the apparent coolness between him and Jordan, the fact that they both visited the bookshop to-day also links up Jordan. And from that, I find that the chain seems to extend through the Jew who keeps the bookshop to Dr. Huxton Rymer, who, being apparently none other than the so-called Professor Andrew Butterfield, makes a complete circle with the suggestions which entered my mind early in the investigation, and brings me right back to the point from where I started.

"Or is it a complete circle? Is it not rather but a portion of the circle, and the second intrusion of Professor Butterfield but a point on the line I am following? I am rather inclined to the latter theory, and, in any event, I shall certainly keep this suggestion in mind."

Thus did Blake sort and analyse the different bits of the puzzle while the train thundered on into Sussex. At each stopping place he kept a cautious eye on the platform, but did not see his man descend. At Horsham he did not get out at once, but opened the door slightly and watched the passengers as they descended. There were only half a dozen or so, and he had no difficulty in recognising Rymer as the latter approached the gate and gave up his ticket.

When he had disappeared, Blake gathered up his books and got out. He passed through the barrier just in time to see Rymer step into a speedy-looking two-seater and drive off. Blake turned to a porter.

"I seem to know that gentleman," he said. "Can you tell me who it is?"

The porter shook his head.

"I have heard his name, but I forget. He lives out a few miles, but comes to the station quite a lot. A professor or doctor, or something like that."

"Ah!" exclaimed Blake, as though suddenly struck by a thought. "Would it be, by any chance, Professor Butterfield?"

"That's it," said the porter. "That's the name."

Blake thanked him, but did not offer a tip. In his shabby condition, he knew that to do so might be to arouse suspicion. Leaving the station, he walked along into the town until he came to the small hotel near West Street. Entering the bar there, he ordered some refreshment, and when he had consumed a portion of it, began his questioning.

His appearance and the books he carried seemed in keeping with his desire to know where Professor Butterfield lived, and the information he sought was readily forthcoming. It seemed that the professor lived about ten miles out, at a place known as Abbey Towers.

That was all Blake required for the moment. He was not ready yet to proceed any farther along that particular line. He had achieved more than he had dared hope for when he left Baker Street. His observation at the bookshop had not only put him in touch with Dr. Huxton Rymer, but it had also enabled him to connect up that gentleman with Professor Andrew Butterfield.

Before taking any steps that might reveal to Rymer that he had been brought within the circle of Blake's investigations, Blake had other things to do in London.

To that end he walked back to the station, and, after a wait of half an hour or so, was lucky enough to get a train back to town.

He arrived at Baker Street to find that Tinker was waiting. The lad examined Blake with a smile as the latter tossed aside his hat and removed his coat, but a curt nod started him on his report.

"You were right in your suspicions about Jordan and Ferguson, guv'nor," he began. "When I went back to the Venetia this afternoon they were in the bar together. I scouted about the place until Browning sent me a tip by Cunningham that both men were leaving the hotel that afternoon. They didn't go together, though. Jordan left first, and Kelly, whom I had put wise, told me that he had given the taxi-driver the address of certain flats in Maida Vale. I was a little undecided whether to go after him or wait for Ferguson, I decided on the latter course, and, as things turned out, it was well that I did. He left about a quarter of an hour after Jordan, and when Kelly told me that he had given the address of the same flats I got a taxi and followed.

"He drove straight there, and paid off the taxi. He carried his bag inside, but the taxi-man took in a small trunk for him. I drove on a little way, and waited, for I knew if Jordan was at the window of the flat, he might see me. When the driver came out, I had my own man signal him. He followed us along, and when he had drawn up I tipped him and questioned him. Well, he took Ferguson's trunk up to a flat on the second floor—the one on the left of the staircase.

"I thought then that I had better question the porter, but it seemed risky to hang about in front of the building, so I sent my driver back to dig him up. It took some time, but eventually he found him. He soon loosened up when I gave him a ten-shilling note, and told me that the flat in question belonged to a Professor Butterfield. It seems, however, that the tenant is very seldom there, and the two who went to the flat this afternoon have sub-leased it from him. That is all."

"And a good deal, too, my lad!" exclaimed Blake, tapping the desk. "Do you know who Professor Butterfield is?"

"No, guv'nor. Who is he?"

"Dr. Huxton Rymer."

"What!" exclaimed Tinker, in amazement. "Rymer? How do you make that out, guv'nor?"

"I didn't know it myself until this afternoon, young 'un," answered Blake. "It was the trail you followed to the bookshop in Old Compton Street that brought the truth to light. I will explain."

Forthwith, Blake related in detail what had happened after he went to the bookshop.

"What you have discovered is but another link in the chain we are trying to follow," he remarked thoughtfully. "There seems little room for doubt now that there exists a very definite connection between Rymer, Jordan, Ferguson, and possibly, the Jew who runs the bookshop. We shall have to find out a little more about him in order to place him exactly. About all we know, so far, is that his name is Samuels, and that he appears to run a perfectly genuine second-hand book business in Old Compton Street."

"Do you think he is a fence, guv'nor?"

"That is what has occurred to me. If he is a fence, then we should have little difficulty in discovering the fact. On the other hand, he may be a specialist, and may not come under that category. But it looks suspicious—very suspicious. I will just see what Van Dorn can tell me."

As he spoke, Blake took the telephone directory and searched until he found the private number of the man whose name he had mentioned, and who was one of the biggest diamond brokers in Hatton Garden. He found that it was in the Hampstead district, and, when he had got through, he finally heard a voice with a distinct Dutch accent speaking.

Van Dorn, Blake knew to be in touch with every phase of the gem-market, both in London and on the Continent, and on more than one occasion he had been able to give Blake valuable information, whereas Blake, on his part, had once handled a case for the broker—handled it in such fashion that Van Dorn still considered Blake almost a magician.

"This is Sexton Blake speaking," said Blake. "I am after a little information, Mr. Van Dorn."

"Oh, it is a long time since I have heard from you, Mr. Blake! What do you wish to know? If I can be of any assistance to you, command me."

"I want to know if you can tell me anything about a man named Samuels who runs a second-hand bookshop in Old Compton Street. It may seem a strange inquiry to put to a diamond broker, but I have reason to believe that he may be interested in gems in an amateurish way."

"Your inquiry is not so strange as it may appear, Mr. Blake. I can tell you that this man is interested in gems."

"Ah! Just how much do you know of that interest, Mr. Van Dorn?"

"Not very much. Samuels has taken an interest in the gem market for several years. I fancy he is very wealthy, and that the bookshop is just a hobby. At any rate, I know that he has at times disposed of some very fine stones, and also that he has bought stones of considerable value. In fact, I have sold him some on several occasions."

"That is most interesting. I wonder if you would extend your kindness still further, Mr. Van Dorn."

"With pleasure. What can I do for you?"

"Have you any engagements for this evening?"

"Nothing particular. I am at home now, and after dinner I intended going on to my club for a rubber. I can easily cancel that."

"Do you think you could get into touch with Mr. Samuels this evening?"

"I fancy so. I have his address somewhere. If he has a telephone, I can ring him up. He lives out in Maida Vale somewhere."

"Ah! Do you remember if it happens to be in the Haverdale Mansions?"

"Hm! I am not certain, but the name has a familiar ring to me."

"What I am going to ask you to do for me, Mr. Van Dorn, is this. I want you, if you will, to get into touch with Mr. Samuels and make him an offer of some stones. You might suggest that you consider them a particular bargain, and you want him to have first refusal. Further, I want you, please, to intimate to him that you might be in the market yourself for some particularly fine stones. Would you do that?"

"Why, certainly! I take it you do not want me to mention that I am doing this for you."

"Assuredly not. It is most essential that my name be kept out of it. I cannot explain my reasons, but it is a matter of considerable importance."

"That is all right. I shall keep mum. This is quite interesting. Am I helping in some sort of a case?"

"To a certain extent—yes," admitted Blake.

"Good! I am your man. Where will I report to you?"

"I shall be at the Venetia Hotel from about eleven o'clock to-night until midnight."

"Right! I shall look you up there."

As Blake hung up the receiver, he turned to Tinker.

"Another little link, my lad. Samuels is no ordinary fence—if he is one at all. But he has at times offered valuable stones for sale, and, moreover, has bought some himself. That is a shrewd move, if he is playing a crooked game: By buying in the open market he establishes the reputation of being an amateur collector—a most valuable impression to create. When we have heard from Van Dorn to-night we may know a little more."

"What next, guv'nor?"

"We shall have an early dinner and, after that, we have a couple of hours work to do in the laboratory."

"What is the game?"

"I practically gave you an outline to-day at lunch, but you didn't seem much interested."

Tinker looked puzzled.

"Do you mean when you were shooting all that high-brow stuff at me?"

Blake smiled.

"Yes. But wait and see."

He went off to his dressing-room then, and not until they were in the laboratory after dinner did Tinker get an inkling as to what Blake was up to. First they dragged out an old wooden chest, that, as far as Tinker could remember, hadn't been opened for a couple of years or so. He watched while Blake rummaged in this for some time, and his gaze grew even more puzzled as he saw what Blake eventually brought to light.

It was an old balloon, made of very thin texture, which Tinker had last seen when Blake was making some air current investigations on the east coast. Between them they tested the fabric to see if it had rotted, but apparently Blake was satisfied, for he laid it on one side with an exclamation of satisfaction.

"Now then, my lad, get an old cigar box and tear the cover off it. Also find a piece of stout cord, say a foot or so in length."

While Tinker went to obey, Blake opened one of the cabinet drawers and searched about until he found a coil of Japanese slow match. He spent a considerable time over this, measuring it with the greatest care. Finally he cut off a length which, uncoiled, measured about three feet, but which, when wound in a close coil, would just fit into the cigar box, which Tinker brought.

Tinker had torn the cover from the box, and now he watched, still unenlightened, while Blake bored a small hole in the centre of the bottom, and four holes in each corner near the top. He next found four lengths of fine wire, each about a foot long. He looped an end of each piece in a corner hole of the box, and brought the free ends together above. These he tied securely, after which he wound the knot with tyre tape.

He left a free length of tyre tape, of about a foot, which, for the time being, he folded lightly. Next, Blake reached for the piece of stout cord which Tinker had brought, and, as he packed the coil of Japanese slow match in the cigar box, it suddenly dawned on Tinker what Blake was up to.

The under end of the slow match Blake pressed through the hole he had bored in the centre of the bottom of the cigar box, and to this end he tied the cord firmly. Then he drew the end of the slow match back through the hole and wound the joining with a short bit of the tape. That done, he straightened up.

"Now do you see, my lad?"

"I see that you are going to attach that cigar box to the old balloon," grunted Tinker. "But I don't follow the idea."

"You will presently. First, however, go into my dressing-room and get that old bag I sometimes use when I go fishing." Tinker did so, and, when he had handed it to Blake, Blake tied the loose end of the thick cord, that projected from the bottom of the cigar box, to the handle.

"Now, my lad," he observed, as he criticised his handiwork, "if you had paid more attention to my discourse at lunch to-day, you might have grasped what I have been attempting to reproduce to-night. In a certain scientific journal, which is, at present, lying on the table in the consulting-room, there is an article on aeronautical science in its relation to future warfare. It is a highly technical paper, and you will be interested to know that it was written by Professor Andrew Butterfield."

"Rymer!"

"Exactly, my lad. Well, to proceed. In that article, the learned professor maintains that vast quantities of explosives can be sent over any given area of country by making use of thousands of small balloons fitted with an automatic timing device, which may be regulated in accordance with the speed of air currents, and wind, as well as the distance to be traversed by the carrying balloon before the bomb is to be let go. His system of control is a very technical system of electrical control, which can be regulated in the desired manner.

"This, that you see before you, is a purely rough hand way of trying to reproduce, very simply, the same result. For instance, you have first the little balloon. When we have filled it with gas, it will easily lift the weight which we shall attach to it. Once it has been filled, I shall attach this free end of tyre tape to the mouth, and the other end is, as you see, attached to the four wires which hold the cigar box on a level keel, so to say. In the box I have packed a length of Japanese slow match, which I have calculated will burn about four hours.

"To the end of that slow match I have tied one end of the thick cord, which you brought, and, to the other, the old bag. When we send the balloon up it will carry this attachment with it, and, if all goes well, then at the end of about four hours, when the slow match has burnt to the end, the glow should eat through the end of the cord which is tied to it, and—voila!—the bag should drop. Now, do you follow me?"

"I follow you all right, guv'nor," said Tinker with a grin. "But when does the balloon go up?"

"To-night from Piccadilly Circus at two o'clock, my lad. If you will study some notes on my desk, you will find that I have ascertained from Stacey, the meteorological expert at Croydon, that air conditions tonight are expected to be practically the same as last night, with the drift in the same direction. Under those favourable conditions, I am going to start our balloon from Piccadilly Circus, and try to ascertain just where this bag will drop four hours later.

"Inside the bag I am going to place a pound note and a request to the effect that the finder will immediately telegraph to Stacey at Croydon just where the bag was picked up, explaining that it is being used as a test for air currents by the aerodrome people there. In addition to that, I am going to hang a little paper lantern beneath the bag—we shall stick it on with tyre tape. In that we shall place a lighted candle for the guidance of Stacey."

"I don't understand that, guv'nor."

"If all goes as I have planned, then at two o'clock to-night, Stacey will he cruising above Piccadilly Circus in a small machine. As soon as we start the balloon we shall let off a magnesium flare, for which he will be watching. Then he is to try and pick up the balloon by the little lantern, which we shall attach, and by cruising through the night in wide circles, will try to follow it. It will be getting light by three o'clock, so if he can keep track of it for the first hour, he should be able to keep it in sight until the bag drops. But in case he loses it, then the note inside should help us to trace it.

"If the slow match works all right, then we should be able to check up what I consider a most important theory, which I have formed in connection with Mrs. Courtlandt's dressing-case, found in Lord Ranborough's plantation. Now, my lad, it is nearly eleven. Let us go on to the Venetia and wait for Van Dorn."

Tinker would fain have questioned Blake at greater length, but he knew he would extract no further information then, so contented himself by assisting Blake to carefully pack up the balloon and the rather ridiculous-looking objects attached to it.

On arriving at the Venetia, Blake left Tinker in the lounge while he went into the writing room and wrote a short note to Mrs. Courtlandt. He knew that the lady would be getting into a state of acute anxiety at not hearing anything from him, and in this state of mind, Blake realised, she might make the whole affair public. That was just what he wanted to avoid, for, once the press got hold of it, his work would be much more difficult, even though the publicity might be of great use to the police.

Blake figured that while the robbery was kept quiet, the thieves would go ahead with their plans, thinking that they had only the regular police forces to watch. But with a general hue and cry raised, Blake knew that the stolen property would at once be started on a rapidly shifting career that would pass it through scores of hands within a few days.

And the more hands it passed through, just so much more difficult would it be for him to trace it.

When he had sent up his note to Mrs. Courtlandt, he rejoined Tinker in the lounge. They sat in a quiet corner until just after half past eleven, when Van Dorn entered. He gazed about him, and finally saw Blake. He came across at once, and, as he dropped into a seat, said:—

"Well, I was able to do as you wished, Mr. Blake. I saw your man this evening."

"What luck?" asked Blake.

"I will tell you exactly what I did. You were quite right in thinking that he lived in the Haverdale Mansions. That was where I called on him. I took along a few very fine stones in my wallet, and, after some conversation, I offered them to him. There was no sale, however, for he informed me that he was not a buyer at present. It seems that he is leaving for the Continent to-morrow. From what he told me, I gather that he is on the track of some exceptionally fine stones that have been smuggled through from Russia.

"At any rate, he said that, on his return, he might have something very exceptional to offer me. I told him, of course, that I was always in the market for high grade stones, but that, under the present depression, I should not be interested in anything else. He then reassured me that, if what he had been told was true, then he was on the track of some of the finest gems that had ever come to Europe. That is all that transpired."

"You have been very kind, Mr. Van Dorn. Did Mr. Samuels say for what part of the Continent he was bound?"

"Yes—Paris."

"And he leaves to-morrow morning?"

"Yes."

"Thank you. That is exactly what I wanted to know."

Van Dorn hesitated for a moment, then he said:—

"Do you mind telling me, Mr. Blake you are interested in the same stones of which Samuels has heard? I mean, are you acting for interests here? Because if you are not already committed, we might arrange for you to act for me."

Blake shook his head regretfully. "I am sorry, Mr. Van Dorn. I should be very glad indeed to oblige you, but I am already committed, and I am not at liberty to divulge the particulars. Will you join me in a whisky and soda?"

Van Dorn agreed, so leaving Tinker in the lounge, they went along to the bar. A quarter of an hour later Mr. Van Dorn departed, and Blake rejoined Tinker.

"How did you know that Samuels lived in the same block of flats to which I followed Jordan and Ferguson?" asked Tinker.

"I didn't," responded Blake. "That was just a long shot. Van Dorn said over the telephone that he was under the impression Samuels lived somewhere in Maida Vale, and I merely suggested the rest. But in the bar I questioned him further, and I have discovered that Samuels lives in the flat on the second floor, which is just opposite that to which you trailed your two men, to-day. That undoubtedly links up Samuels with Jordan and Ferguson, as well as with Rymer. I think, my lad, that we have struck the right nest."

"What do you suppose Samuels is going to Paris for, guv'nor?"

"We can only surmise, but I feel convinced it has something to do with the missing jewels, my lad. What Van Dorn has been able to tell us is of the utmost value. For instance, we know that, while Samuels is nearly always ready for a good bargain in good stones, he is not inclined that way at the present time. On the contrary, he hints at being on the track of some very exceptional jewels, and leads Van Dorn to believe that they have been smuggled through from Russia.

"He follows that up by suggesting that, on his return from the Continent, he may be able to offer some of them to Van Dorn. Now we know that the very greatest care will be needed in disposing of the Courtlandt jewels. They are known the world over to all the leading gem specialists, and no ordinary fence could ever dispose of them. On the other hand, there are ways and means which a man like Samuels could make use of. For instance, it is true that there have been some very fine gems smuggled through from Russia and Austria, and that fact makes it easier to place the Courtlandt collection, if it be split up, than if these other stones had not also been thrown on the market.

"By patient work, a clever fence could dispose of a few of the Courtlandt stones at a time and, perhaps, buy back some of the Russian stones until he had so intermixed them all that detection would be almost an impossibility. That, in my opinion, is what will be attempted, and if we are to recover the Courtlandt collection, then we must run them to earth before they are separated.

"Then you think Samuels is the fence who will try that?"

"I don't know—yet. But we have a good two hours before us before we send up the balloon, Tinker. We shall drive back to Baker Street and pick up one or two things. Then we shall try to discover just what Mr. Samuels is up to."

"In what way, guv'nor?"

Blake placed his hand over his mouth.

"We will turn burglars on our own account, Tinker. I want to have a look at the room behind the bookshop, and, if possible, to make an examination of the interior of Mr. Samuel's safe. Now, come on—we have only two hours in which to work."

CHAPTER 8.   A Daring Burglary and the Startling Result— Curious Proceedings in Piccadilly Circus—A Tense Moment for Blake.

IT did not take Blake long to choose what he required at Baker Street. From his own examination of the bookshop premises that afternoon, he knew that it would be unwise to attempt to force an entry from the front, unless all other means failed. He knew that it was a very old three-storey building, the two upper floors of which, he concluded, were probably rented out as rooms or small apartments.

The ground floor he knew to be entirely occupied by Samuels, and, what he had at first concluded must be living quarters at the back, he now figured probably consisted of Samuel's private office and perhaps an extra room which might be used for the storage of old books.

At any rate, that was the assumption he was going on, and when Tinker stated that he knew a small alley ran at the rear, Blake determined to make his first attempt there. The lower windows at the back might be heavily barred, and that would complicate things and perhaps force him to try the front, for he had only two hours in which to carry out his suddenly conceived plan.

It was altogether likely that any wall at the rear would be high and protected by iron spikes, but that was an obstacle soon surmounted. Therefore he chose only a light but strong silken ladder with two thin iron hooks at one end, a light jemmy, a bunch of skeleton keys, a file, a screwdriver, a piece of coarse brown paper, a fine saw with some oil, a little putty, a small phial of thick molasses-like liquid, and, lastly, rubber gloves for himself and Tinker.

Almost every item of the kit had come from a collection that had been presented to Blake by a one-time notorious criminal, and each article of metal was of the finest temper. The outfit had been that light-fingered gentleman's most treasured possession.

Neither of them made much attempt at disguise, excepting to choose for Blake a wide brimmed soft felt hat, which pulled well down over his eyes, and for Tinker a cap, the peak of which served the same purpose. Thus equipped, they started out, and Tinker drove the Grey Panther at high speed until they turned off Shaftesbury Avenue.

Their immediate objective was a small garage just off Old

Compton Street, which Tinker knew well, and where the car would be left until needed. It was now past midnight, and, while there was still plenty of movement in the more-frequented thoroughfares, the little side-street off Old Compton was practically deserted.

The door of the garage was closed, and while Tinker banged on it Blake walked along a short distance and stood in the shadow. When he was joined by Tinker the latter took the lead, and, after a couple of turnings, turned into a narrow alley that was completely deserted.

"This is the lane of which I told you, guv'nor," whispered the lad as they felt their way along. "It serves the buildings on Old Compton Street, or, at least, some of them, and those on the other street to our left. We ought to be able to pick up the bookshop easy enough, for it stands between two lower buildings."

They kept along until suddenly Tinker touched Blake's arm.

"That looks like it," he whispered.

Blake muttered something softly, and, as they came directly at the rear of the house which stood up a little from the two that flanked it, they stopped. Tinker had brought a torch with him, and, at a word from Blake he pressed the switch and flashed it over the high wall against which they were standing.

It was not of wood, as Blake had half anticipated, but of brick, with long, sharp spikes set at intervals in the joints. It was not topped by broken bottles, as he had feared on first seeing it.

There was a heavy wooden gate, also topped by spikes, but a brief examination of this showed them that it would be a very long and risky business to force it. But Blake did decide on making his attempt there, instead of at some point along the wall. While Tinker kept a sharp look-out Blake took out the little silken ladder, and, after a couple of casts, managed to get the hooks caught on the top of the gate. Then he drew on his rubber gloves, and, feeling cautiously for a toe-hold on the cord rungs, he began to mount.

It was slow work, for the reason that the ladder was not equipped with any device to keep it out from the wall. Tinker helped a little by pulling it out as Blake mounted higher, but even then it was not easy.

At last, however, he reached the top, where he balanced himself carefully, for he knew what would happen if he should fall and if his coat should catch in the spikes. It was a good seven-foot drop to the other side, but, after trying to pierce the gloom beneath him, Blake swung round and lowered his body until he was hanging the full extent of his arms. Then he dropped.

It was only a very short distance, and he landed with scarcely a sound on the other side. He stood waiting until Tinker should signal that he had reached the top of the gate. A soft hiss came a few seconds later, and into Blake's outstretched arms dropped the ladder. Then there was a faint scraping sound as Tinker's toes slithered down against the wood. Blake eased him to the ground, and took out his own torch.

By the light he saw that they were in a yard of sorts, and not over clean at that. It was littered with old barrels and boxes and apparently was used principally as an overflow place by the several tenants of the building. Blake led the way across until they were close to the wall of the house.

There were three windows there, and, as he had feared, those at which he first directed the light were barred; but, as he brought the torch to bear on the last one on his left, he saw that it was not barred. A closer examination revealed, however, that it was secured by what seemed to be a very strong catch on the inside, and a very few moments' effort with a thin steel blade proved that the catch was not of the type that could be pressed back.

The blind was down, and they could not see what sort of a room was on the other side. But, somehow, Blake felt certain it must communicate with some part of the premises occupied by Samuels, and he determined to force the window without further delay. It was not a difficult matter for such practised hands.

First he took out the little phial of sticky brown liquid, then the piece of coarse brown paper. Smearing the glass and the paper with the brown mess, he stuck the paper on the glass. Then he took out one of the fine tools which he had brought with him. In less than sixty seconds he had cut a deep, circular incision around the paper.

Then he took hold of the paper, and gave the circle of glass one single sharp tap. The next instant the piece had come away in his fingers, and this he handed to Tinker who immediately broke it in half and trust it in the side-pocket of his coat.

The hole which Blake had cut was large enough to admit his hand easily. It was likewise up near the upper frame of the lower sash, so that it was now a comparatively simple matter for him to thrust in his hand, get his fingers on the catch, and force it back. Then, with the jemmy, he pressed very gently beneath the lower frame of the sash.

The sill gave him a good leverage, and, inch by inch, the sash rose.

When he had lifted it a foot or so Blake desisted in order to raise the blind, then Tinker's torch was brought into play, revealing before them a room literally half filled with old lumber and books. It was exactly what Blake had hoped for and now as he saw a door on his right, he guessed that it must be a means of access into the private room from which he had seen Rymer emerge.

Blake raised the sash still more, and climbed easily over the sill, followed by Tinker. They both dropped softly to the floor, and, with Tinker's torch lighting the way, they made for the door. It was an ordinary wooden door, but had been locked on the other side.

Blake inserted a skeleton key, only to find that the key had been left in on the other side. He next attacked it with a very line pair of tweezers, and kept poking and twisting away at it until the tweezers suddenly went in deep and a soft tinkle came from the other side of the door,

"Got it!" he breathed, "Now for the skeleton, Tinker!''

This time the skeleton met with no obstruction, and, under Blake's coaxing, the bolt soon went back. He turned the handle, and, opening the door; stepped into Samuel's private office.

The room was rather untidy, and a good many old books were scattered about. The furniture was very old, but a remarkably substantial and modern-looking safe stood in one corner. Samuels' desk had been placed near one of the barred windows, with the chair so that Samuels would sit with his back to the light.

The big safe was just between this and the wall. Signing for Tinker to keep the torch going, Blake strode across to the desk and made a brief examination of things there. Apparently he found nothing or interest, for he soon turned his attention to the safe.

He was just bending over it when suddenly a clock overhead struck one, and so startlingly did the sound come on the silence that Tinker gave a jump and almost dropped the torch. Blake clucked with impatience, and gestured sharply for the lad to be more careful.

Now he took from his pocket a small microphone, which he attached to the safe close beside the combination. After that he placed the ear-tubes in his ears and, taking hold of the knob with his rubber-covered fingers, began to puzzle out the cipher.

The combination was of the American numbered type, and Blake went to work at it on the assumption that it would be of the standard four-turn description—that is, a single turn in one direction, a double turn in the opposite direction, a triple turn back the first way, and a quadruple turn, as the second. In order to check up the cipher, he would have to find out at least three of the numbers before attempting to locate the final one, at which the numbers would fall back. And to do this was a very ticklish piece of work, needing the utmost silence.

Therefore, while he worked away at the knob, listening through the tubes of the microphone for the faint sounds that would tell him when he had reached one of the ciphers, Tinker, who held the torch, scarcely breathed. He watched tensely while Blake turned this way and that, while he seemed to pause on a number, then give the knob a swift twirl, and start all over again.

In this way he laboured at it until suddenly his fingers came to a rest, and even Tinker heard the faint click as the tumblers fell back,

Blake then removed the ear-tubes from his ears, and replaced the microphone in his pocket. Next, he took hold of the big nickle handle of the safe door, and turned it hard to the right. Released by the locking combination, the thick bolts now slid back smoothly enough, and the next second Blake had dragged the door open, leaving the interior of the safe at their mercy. It had been as nice a piece of work as the slickest cracksman could have pulled off.

But if Sexton Blake had expected all his stealthy labours to put him on the track of something that would confirm the suspicions that had been roused in his mind against Samuels, the book dealer, half an hour was sufficient to tell him that he would not find it in that safe. It was a perfectly respectable safe in every way.

Inside, it was divided into several narrow partitions, in which account books had been placed. A very brief examination of these showed that the entries referred to perfectly genuine transactions in the book business. In the centre of the safe were two cash drawers, which Blake prised open. In one was a bundle of banknotes, with a few sheets of memoranda unquestionably referring to the amounts of the notes.

In the second drawer was some silver and a few pieces of gold— rare enough in these days. The upper half of the safe was divided into more partitions, in which were several bundles of documents—fire insurance policies, a few Government bonds, some shares, and a bundle of private letters, which had no bearing on what Blake was after. Nor was there the faintest suggestion of a secret compartment.

It was simply an honest to goodness safe, and given up to a thoroughly genuine business. When Blake realised that this was so, he closed the two drawers and swung the heavy door until it rumbled into place. Then he pressed the bolts home, and gave the knob of the combination a whirl.

He was still squatting before the door, gazing at the knob in a puzzled way, when suddenly both he and Tinker grew rigid as a sound reached them. It came from the direction of the outer shop, and when, a second later, they heard the sound of a voice, Tinker released the switch of the torch, and like two shadows he and Blake stole back to the lumber-room.

Blake had no time to replace the key in the door, for, as he had entered the room, he had picked it up and dropped it in his pocket. All they could do was to shut the door and await events. They had not long to wait, for Blake had barely released the handle when they heard someone enter the adjoining room.

A click sounded as the lights were switched on. Blake bent down and placed his eye against the keyhole. At first he could only make out the outlines of the desk, but presently a figure blurred his view, and as the man turned Blake recognised Samuels.

"Now, what does he want here at this hour of the night?" he thought, as he watched intently. "Perhaps he has forgotten something that he wants to take to Paris with him. Hallo! What is he up to now?"

Blake grew tense, and gave Tinker a cautious touch as he saw Samuels turn and stare towards the door, behind which they crouched. He stood thus for some seconds; then, with a gesture of decision, he took out an automatic pistol and laid it on the desk. The next moment he walked straight towards the door. Blake gave Tinker another urgent touch, and waited for the door to open. But it did not do so.

Samuels came to a stop just before reaching it, and Blake could not see what he was doing, for he bulked so close to the keyhole now that Blake's view was almost entirely cut off. Soon the bulk moved aside, and Blake could make out that Samuels was standing close to the wall near the door.

Some minutes passed, during which faint sounds reached the listeners; then came a louder thud than any of the others—a thud that gave Blake a sudden idea. Following that, his view was again blurred, but only for a few seconds, for Samuels returned to the desk.

Standing there, he gazed slowly about the room, his hand resting close to the pistol as he did so. Then from his pocket he took a flat paper packet. He placed this on the desk, and bent over it in such a way that Blake could not see what he was doing. It appeared as if he might be examining the contents, and, as this thought came to Blake, he bent his head close to Tinker and whispered the one word: "Now!"

Tinker moved a little as Blake turned the handle of the door with infinite caution. Samuels was undoubtedly deeply engrossed in his occupation, for he did not lift his head as Blake slowly drew the door open. Then for a single moment Blake stood poised on the threshold; the next instant he had sprung across the room like a panther, and before the startled Jew could do more than half-turn his head, Blake was upon him, one arm locked tight under Samuel's chin to prevent an outcry, the other pinioning his arm in a grip of steel.

The Jew, fat and out of condition, was as helpless as a child in the powerful arms of the detective. Blake forced him slowly forward over the desk until his face was close to the blotting-pad.

Only then did Blake get a glimpse of what had held the Jew's interest, and now he saw a heap of glittering gems before him that made even his gaze widen. No wonder Samuels had not heard them.

While he held his victim over the desk Blake made a gesture towards Tinker, and his lips noiselessly formed a word. Tinker caught his meaning, and jerked out his handkerchief. In one corner was his initial, but this he removed by the simple process of stuffing the corner of the handkerchief between his teeth and tearing it free.

The shred he put in his pocket, then he bound the handkerchief tightly round the Jew's eyes. When he had knotted it securely, he caught Samuels by the heels, and together they laid him on the floor. Tinker then got some bits of cord from a parcel of books in one corner, and in three minutes the Jew was trussed, hand and foot.

Now Blake took a hand, and, using the Jew's own tie and handkerchief, gagged him. Following that, he took out the little piece of putty he had brought. He had anticipated that he might have to use this on the window, but it had not been necessary. He broke off two small portions and stuffed one in each of Samuels' ears. That done, he got to his feet.

"Bound, blind, deaf, and dumb," he murmured, in a low tone that could only reach Samuels' ears as an indistinct rumble. "He will be all right for a while, at least."

"My aunt, guv'nor!" exclaimed Tinker, in an excited whisper.

"Look at these!" — indicating the gems on the desk which he had just spotted.

Blake's answer was to fold the paper over them and coolly drop the packet in his pocket. Then he bent over their victim, and, thrusting his hand in his pocket, took out a small bunch of keys.

Tinker watched with interest as Blake crossed the room to the corner near the door, behind which they had been concealed. Against the wall was a big pile of old books. Blake removed a few from the top, and then motioned for Tinker to approach.

"That is why we didn't find anything in the safe," he said, as he pointed at a small strong box inserted in the wall.

"Quite a clever idea, that. Not one burglar in a hundred would think of looking behind these old books. He would confine himself entirely to the safe. Now, let us see if there is anything else here."

He tried key after key, until at last he found the right one. But as he swung back the little door he gave a shrug of disappointment, for the interior of the strong box was absolutely empty. Blake closed and locked the door, and replaced the books. Then he stuffed the keys back in Samuels' pocket. He glanced up at the clock, and saw that it was a quarter to two. As he noted this, he made a curt gesture to Tinker.

"Out with that light, my lad, and let's get out of this. Wait! On second thoughts we will leave the light on. As Samuels came in he spoke to someone. It must have been the constable on the beat. A glimmer of the light may show under the door. Better leave it. Come on."

With that, Blake led the way into the lumber-room, the door of which he closed. They slipped out through the window, which Tinker drew down after him. Then they crossed the yard to the gate. There they dragged a barrel across, and, after casting the silken ladder, it was a comparatively easy matter to swing over and drop to the lane on the other side.

As before, Tinker dropped the ladder down to Blake, who rolled it up and stuffed it in his pocket. Then, keeping close to the wall, they made for the garage.

It was just two o'clock when Tinker drove the Grey Panther into the kerb in front of the Venetia. Blake had already arranged with Kelly, the commissionaire, about a very necessary adjunct to the experiment he had planned for that night. This was a compressed cylinder of gas, and, as Kelly was off duty during the night, it had been arranged that he should come along with them.

Kelly was on hand, waiting, and eager to get started. He didn't know exactly what Blake planned doing, but he had a fervent admiration for the criminologist, and was highly flattered to be in on something which he shrewdly suspected had some bearing on the Courtlandt affair.

He climbed in after stowing the heavy cylinder in the back, and, swinging the car round, Tinker drove back to the Circus. They drew into the kerb a little way down Lower Regent Street, where it was dark, and, covered by Tinker and Kelly, Blake got his apparatus out from under the seat and went over it bit by bit.

When he was satisfied that it was in order, he gave the sign to Kelly, who forced the end of the cylinder into the mouth of the miniature balloon, and turned the cock. Immediately there was a sudden hissing, and, as the bag began to fill and expand, a constable ran hotfooted towards them.

"Here, what's all this?" he began, but stopped as Kelly whispered hoarsely: "Stow that, Bill. We don't want all the night-hawks round. You know me, and you know Mr. Sexton Blake and his assistant here. This is just a little experiment of ours."

Blake smiled at the important lilt in Kelly's voice, but it had the desired effect, and the constable stood watching with puzzled interest as the balloon swelled slowly until the cloth was taut, and had a spread of about six feet in diameter. It was pulling upwards now, with more strength than one would have thought, so Blake gave the mouth to Kelly to hold, while he sealed it.

Then he tested all his taped joinings, and, finally prepared his little paper lantern. This he stuck to the bottom of the bag with tyre tape, and, when that was done, gave the hanging objects to Tinker to guard.

Blake now stepped out into the street and stood listening. Almost at that same instant, a faint droning sound reached them. It grew louder and louder, until it seemed to be directly overhead. Then it grew fainter and almost died away, but only for a moment, before once more growing in volume.

"Stacey right on the dot, and cruising overhead," muttered Blake. "I will give him the flare now."

He strode back to the car, and, after a word to Tinker and Kelly warning them to be ready, he took from one of the door pockets a small sheet of zinc and a strip of magnesium flare. He returned to the centre of the street, and, holding the zinc with the magnesium strip on it, lighted a match. The next instant there was a blinding flash as the flare went up.

Blake was half blinded for a moment and stumbled as he made his way back to the car. He tossed the zinc sheet into the bottom of the car, and, hurrying round to the other side, hastily lighted the candle which he had stuck inside the paper lantern.

He had just touched a match to the slow burning fuse when there came a loud report overhead, and, a moment later, a swish as a Verey light shot up into the sky and broke in a beautiful curve.

"Stacey saw your flash," exclaimed Tinker.

Blake nodded. "Come on," he ordered. "We will send it up from the middle of the street. Mind the bag, Kelly, and don't get those tapes twisted, Tinker."

The three of them carried the apparatus out until they were in the middle of the road.

"Now, I will count three," went on Blake. "At the three, Kelly, you release the bag. The very second you feel the pull, Tinker, let go the box and the bag.

I will see that the paper lantern follows without being jerked off. Now then—one, two, THREE!"

As Blake jerked out the last word, Kelly let the bag slip gently from his hands. It sprang upwards, and from Tinker's loose hold the cigar box went next, followed by the old leather handbag.

As Blake's keen eyes saw it slipping away, he balanced the little paper lantern to a nicety, and the next instant, the whole apparatus was soaring swiftly up between the buildings that lined the street. The policeman had now joined them, and all eyes were strained upwards, following the little light that dangled from the bottom.

Blake's great fear was that it would foul some of the buildings, but as they watched, they saw it lift far above, then, as it was caught in the upper air currents, it soared away from their view.

Still they stood watching, and when a second report rang out, and a second scattering shower of fire spread across the sky, Blake knew that Stacey had picked up the little light. A few persons were now beginning to gather, and as the last thing Blake wanted was to attract the attention of the curious, he led the way back to the car.

With a word of good-night to the constable, who, incidentally, immediately went along to scatter the curious, they piled into the car, and Tinker drove off swiftly towards Pall Mall. He drove into the Mall, and kept on until just near the statue at the upper end. There he turned, and switched off the engine.

Thus they sat listening to the drone of Stacey's machine, which could still be heard overhead. But if the little balloon was there they could not see its light at such a height, and so, when the drone of the aeroplane had dually died away, Blake gave the signal to drive back to the Venetia,

On their arrival there Blake detained Kelly.

"Tinker and I are coming in, Kelly, and I have something else for you to do tonight."

"Why, sure, Mr. Blake. What is it?"

"I want you to take a note up to Mrs. Stuyvesant Courtlandt. See that you give it into her own hand. You had better telephone her room first, and tell her that you are coming up. That will give her a chance to throw on some wraps. When she reads the note, she will answer either the one word 'yes' or 'no.' Then return to me in the lounge. While you are telephoning, I will scribble a note."

Blake wrote his note at a small table in the lounge, and had sealed it ready, by the time Kelly returned.

"She says to bring it up," he announced. Blake nodded and handed the envelope to him. In five minutes Kelly was back.

"She says 'yes,' " he said.

"Good, Kelly. Come on, Tinker. We will go up by the staircase." And when they had left Kelly behind, Blake added grimly: "We shall soon know now, my lad, whether we were justified or not in handling Samuels as we did."

CHAPTER 9. Rymer Caught Napping—The New Partner— The Pact.

IF Sexton Blake had been busy since his arrival in London from Lord Ranborough's place, Professor Andrew Butterfield, otherwise Dr. Huxton Rymer, had been no less occupied.

When first approached by Thurlow Jordan, and asked to outline a scheme by which the Courtlandt jewels might be "lifted," it will be recalled that Rymer had consented on two conditions.

The first was that Jordan should hand over the amount of the "fee" in Treasury notes before receiving the plan, and the second was a condition that the jewels, if secured, should be disposed of through a fence whom Rymer should name. In that second condition was the "nigger in the woodpile," so to say.

Rymer was extremely dubious of the ability of Jordan and Ferguson to carry the plan through, even though it looked logical enough as he outlined it. He had not the slightest doubt that he himself would have been able to bring it off, but he was not very highly impressed with Jordan. He knew little of Ferguson, but he was perfectly aware that great coolness and daring were essential. If Ferguson could supply that, then there was a chance.

That Ferguson did supply the necessary qualities he discovered when a short code telegram reached him on the morning following the robbery. That telegram caused him to rub his hands with an unholy sense of anticipation, for now was when the main part of his plan would come into effect—at least as far as he was concerned.

Dr. Huxton Rymer had not the faintest intention that Jordan and Ferguson should get away with such a wonderful haul without a very large share of the spoils coming to him. That was what his second condition ensured, for, if Jordan and Ferguson carried out that condition, then the disposal of the stones would be controlled by Rymer through the fence he had named.

He had already given the name of the fence to the two crooks, and the visit of, first, Jordan, and then Ferguson to Samuels in Old Compton Street, was the result. Rymer had little fear that either Jordan or Ferguson would dare to try and double-cross him. He had them absolutely at his mercy, and they knew it; whereas, they had absolutely nothing on him.

That was as it should be, according to Rymer, for, while he was not averse to coming in on the spoils, he was determined, if possible, to keep quite clear of any police entanglements. Another thing gave him a hold over the two crooks.

At the time he had outlined a plan for them, it will be remembered that he also provided Jordan with certain things to be used in connection therewith, and which Jordan had taken with him to London in his car. These things had been smuggled into the hotel in his luggage, but, after the trick had been turned, it was necessary to get rid of them without delay.

They dared make no attempt to leave the hotel early or to attempt to remove their luggage. Rymer had warned them most strongly about this, and when Jordan saw Sexton Blake in the Venetia on the morning after the robbery he was quite shrewd enough to guess that the famous criminologist was probably already working on the case.

When the newspapers, later in the day, made no mention of the robbery, then he and Ferguson had felt positive this was so. But, as planned by Rymer, they had succeeded not only in removing the apparatus safely, but they had managed, as well, to get the booty away and place it in what they considered a safe place. That was the reason for their visit to Old Compton Street.

In the meantime Rymer had been in communication with Samuels, and, following that, had come up to town early in the afternoon. Hence it was that Blake saw him emerge from Samuels' private room. If Blake could but have overheard what passed between the two men, and if he could but have guessed what a cunning camouflage was the huge book which Professor Butterfield had carried away with him, he would not have terminated his chase at Horsham.

But, of course, Blake did not know this, and he realised that to act precipitately might endanger the success of the whole case. Therefore, he was forced to proceed cautiously, picking up thread after thread, while, at Abbey Towers, Rymer was preparing to heave another brick into the machinery.

Blake's suspicions of Samuels were more than well-founded. No more cunning or cautious fence existed in all Europe than the dealer in second-hand books. What gave him more protection than anything was the fact that the business was run on perfectly genuine lines.

That had been obvious to Blake. Nor did Samuels make the mistake of dealing with the raggle-taggle of crookdom. On the contrary, it was only a few criminals of the calibre of Rymer who even guessed that Samuels acted as an agent, and, even then, it was only when an occasional "job" of great importance was brought off.

Blake had struck the exact truth when he guessed that Samuels' buying and selling at different times in the open market was but a very subtle plan to establish for himself the reputation of being an amateur collector of fine stones; and, indeed, so was he regarded in Hatton Garden, as well as in Paris and Amsterdam. Nevertheless, both he and Rymer realised full well that to break up and dispose of the Courtlandt collection would be the most difficult problem Samuels had had to solve for many years.

Firstly, the majority of the individual stones were well known to most of the European specialists, and, secondly, it stood to reason that, sooner or later, there must be the very dickens of a hue and cry after them. Enormous rewards would be offered, and every dealer, legitimate and otherwise, would be on the look-out for them.

On the other hand, conditions were more favourable than they had been for some years, owing to the tremendous influx of smuggled family heirlooms from Russia and Austria. London had received a large quantity of these, and Paris was full of them, at bargain prices. Moreover, it was summer, and at the present time there were more wealthy American and South American tourists in Europe than ever before.

They would form the eventual destination of the stones, but there was a difficult road to travel first. Therefore, it had been decided that the larger pieces should be taken by Rymer to Abbey Towers, where, in his well-equipped laboratory, he would remove the stones from their gold and platinum settings, and melt down the metal.

The smaller part of the collection would be handled immediately by Samuels, who would leave the following day, and there put into effect the plan they had formed to dispose of them. Rymer, as soon as he had carried out his work, would also proceed to Paris.

With that decision, Rymer had returned to Horsham, and as Blake saw him leave the bookshop with the large book he had apparently purchased he never guessed that, while the edges of the pages were genuine enough, the whole inside had been cut out, forming, when closed, a large receptacle, in which a considerable quantity of jewels could be carried.

It may well be imagined that Rymer was in an exceedingly

cheerful mood as he entered Abbey Towers. And, indeed, well he might be, for had he not under his arm jewels worth almost any figure one could name?

Jordan and Ferguson had received a heavy cash advance from Samuels, and, of course, they would receive more when the stones were finally disposed of, but the greater part of the money received would go into the pockets of Samuels and Rymer. Rymer would see to that, and the two younger crooks would be helpless to protest.

Things looked very bright indeed for the "Crime Adviser," but he had been in the Towers less than twenty minutes when he received a shock that at first made him feel as if he had taken a plunge into icy water. And that shock came about in this way.

On entering his library, Rymer laid his big book on the table and locked the door. He next crossed to the door leading to the laboratory, where he drew aside the concealing curtain and inserted the key.

Leaving the door open, he went back to the table, picked up the "book," and passed into the laboratory. It was his intention to place the loot in one of the strong steel cabinets ranged against the wall at the far end, and to start to work on the setting immediately after an early dinner.

But as he passed the centre dissecting-table, and the light from the glass dome overhead struck him with its mellow shafts, he could not resist the impulse to have just one gloating look at the loot. He laid the book on the table, and swiftly untied the cord. Removing the brown-paper wrapper, he lifted the cover of the book, and then gave a deep sigh of sheer joy as he gazed at the twinkling gems before him.

To anyone the sight would have been spellbinding, but to one of Rymer's temperament it acted more as a potent drug than anything else. He was completely engrossed, utterly enthralled. His eyes narrowed, and the pupils dilated in nervous reaction. His breathing was short and laboured. His face was pale with emotion, and his long, nervous fingers twitched spasmodically. He was drunk with treasure lust.

At last he gave a sharp exclamation, and lifted his head as his hand went out to close the cover. Then he stood pertified at what he saw, for standing on the threshold of the door that led to the library, and which he had left open, was the housemaid, Mary Trent, regarding him with a mocking smile that made Rymer shiver.

He was still standing paralysed at the shock of the discovery, when, with a sinuous, gliding movement, she reached the table. Rymer threw on all his control, and made to close the cover; but not before the girl had caught a glimpse of the dazzling contents. Then she smiled again.

"Put them away, professor," she said softly. "Then come into the library. The time has arrived when we must talk."

Like a man in a dream, Rymer turned and did her bidding. All the same, it was not from the shock that he now moved like an automaton, but because he was trying to figure out exactly what he should do. He knew that, from a physical point of view, it would be simple enough for him to take care of the girl; but he was all at sea as to just what her intentions were.

He considered the possibility of her being a police-spy, but something in the quality of her mocking smile told him this was not the case. Then who was she? He had already been faintly curious about her. She had always struck him as something of an enigma, but until then he had thought it was probably because she was hardly the type of ordinary housemaid.

There was an assurance of bearing and a quality of voice and accent which were more of the educated and cultured classes than of the circles in which she now moved. At any rate, he thought, as he locked away the "book," he would soon know, and when he did he could decide just how he should deal with her.

Nevertheless, it revealed that the professional veneer that he had so carefully spread over the personality of Dr. Huxton Rymer had been scratched—and that, under his own rooftree.

Mary Trent preceded him to the library, and, after coolly selecting one of Rymer's cigarettes, seated herself in one of the easy chairs. She waited until Rymer had dropped into the chair at his desk, then she smiled again.

"Well, professor, I have solved the puzzle at last."

"What do you mean?" he asked cautiously.

"Just what I say. Ever since I have been here I have been puzzled about you. If you will permit me to say so, you struck me as being altogether too young and—er— red-blooded to be content to spend the rest of your life in dry and dusty scientific research. On the other hand, it seemed that I must be wrong, for I took the trouble to read your papers as they were published, and they were brilliant— extremely brilliant, professor."

Rymer relaxed a little under the girl's subtle flattery, but did not commit himself to any remark.

"But still, things were inconsistent," she went on, after studying the end of her cigarette for a few seconds. "In the first place, you are a gourmet—you have a critical discrimination of food and wines that one does not find in the general run of research students. They are usually too engrossed in their work to care what they eat and drink. You also choose only the finest brands of cigars and cigarettes.

"Then, again, some of your visitors were not the sort that one would expect a research professor to find congenial. For instance, there is Mr. Thurlow Jordan. Now that young man wouldn't understand the simplest phrases on your papers. You see, I happened to know something about him. And what I know made me still more curious when I found that he and you spent several apparently very congenial hours together. I decided then, professor, that it would be worth while keeping my eyes and ears open.

"Therefore, when you showed signs of repressed excitement this morning as you were leaving for Horsham, I decided that something quite out of the ordinary had happened, and I wondered if that something might not be in connection with the side of your nature that puzzled me so. Do not think, professor, that I am suggesting for a single moment that you are a species of Dr. Jekyll and Mr. Hyde. But it was curious.

"Well, before your return I slipped in here and concealed myself behind the heavy window curtains. I heard you lock the door, and I even peeped out as you went into the laboratory. You know the rest. You may be Professor Butterfield. That you are certainly a very brilliant scientist is certain. But the other part, dear professor, the ether part—that is where Mary Trent comes in."

While Rymer had listened in wooden silence to her words, his mind was working swiftly, and as she made each point he had to admit to himself that she possessed a penetration of mind that he had certainly not credited her with.

Her point on the food and wines had evoked his admiration, and her manner of handling the whole subject suggested to him that her words were not the prelude to a threat, but the preface to a demand. That was what he wanted to get out of her.

"You have considerable powers of observation," he said slowly. "I, on my part, might suggest that if I, as a professor, strike you as being a little inconsistent at times, you, as a housemaid, are even more of an anomaly, although, I must confess, that your work is very efficient."

She made him a mock bow and smiled again.

"Thank you, professor. It is good to know that I have given satisfaction as a housemaid. But are we not getting a little away from the subject? You see, while I am quite willing to admit that I have not always been a housemaid, I have nothing so embarrassing to explain as the possession of gems worth a fabulous amount, and which are kept concealed in a camouflaged book."

"Just who are you? And what is it you want?" asked Rymer, eyeing her from an entirely different angle than at any previous time.

"Who am I? Just Mary Trent. What do I want? I want a share in the proceeds of those stones, professor."

"But if I say that my having those stones in my keeping is capable of a very ordinary explanation?"

She laughed outright.

"You are forgetting that I was watching you as you examined them, professor." And Rymer knew that in the emotion he had shown he had revealed the truth to her penetrating mind.

"Tell me in detail just what you want," he said at last.

The girl sat up straight.

"I want, as I said, a share in whatever is realised in the disposal of those stones. I have seen quite enough to know that they are no ordinary jewels, and I know, too, that they have only recently come into your possession. I want a full and frank partnership. I want to know where they came from, and how you propose disposing of them.

"On my part, I can bring qualities that will make me an asset to you. I have brains, and know how to use them. I can carry off any role which it might be necessary at times for me to play. You would have no need to feel nervous of me in whatever circle it might be necessary for me to move. Moreover, I, as a woman would have access to information that would be denied to you as a man. Together, professor, we should go far."

Rymer gazed into her eyes searchingly.

"If I knew whether I could trust you —" he began.

She returned his gaze steadily, then, just before her lids drooped, Rymer glimpsed a flame that leaped into her eyes in sudden revelation.

"You can trust me—completely," she whispered.

And Rymer knew that she spoke the truth.

"I accept," he said, as he rose and laid his hand on hers. "Come here to-night after dinner when the housekeeper has retired. I will tell you all. Afterwards it is necessary for me to work all night, for I must leave for Paris to-morrow. You shall help me."

Her hand trembled a little under his, then she withdrew it and rose. For a moment their eyes again met, then she gave him a little nod and walked to the door. Five minutes later she returned, bringing a tea-tray; and not the closest eye could have detected anything out of the ordinary in the attitude of the pretty and extremely efficient housemaid towards the bespectacled professor.

And Rymer kept his word. Late that night they sat together in the library, while Rymer told her who he was and exactly how the Courtlandt jewels had come into his possession. As the girl smoked and listened quietly to the details, one would never have guessed that she was other than an intimate friend or relation of the professor to whom he was discoursing on some scientific subject.

Gone was the badge of the domestic, and, in place of it was a simple, but exquisitely fashioned frock that even Rymer knew could only have come from Paris. Gone, too, was the cap, and now her thick, soft, hair gleamed attractively under the light. Rymer realised that she had not boasted. She could carry off any role with the ease which is only born and cannot be acquired.

From time to time, she asked a pertinent question, but mostly, she just listened, nodding her head in approval. When he had finished, she said:

"Your plan of splitting up the stones is good. Also, no time should be lost in melting down the settings. But you will have need for care in trying to smuggle the stones across to France. I have a plan which I think would make that easier."

"What is it?" asked Rymer, admiring the speed at which her mind worked.

"It is this. You are known as Professor Butterfield. Very well. Now all professors are considered generally as rather simple folk, about the ordinary affairs of life, and as persons who need looking after. That, of course, is a ridiculous point of view, but it exists nevertheless. It will be an asset to you. You have said you intend flying to Paris. In that case, I suggest that you take me along as your amanuensis, I can easily carry off the part for I know shorthand.

"I think it would be wise, too, if you were to wear a pair of slightly tinted spectacles, and to act as if you were very short-sighted. That will give me an excuse for taking you by the arm in a protective sort of way. With a touch of helplessness about the details of travelling, I do not think the Customs officials will pay much attention to you. You can carry your book under your arm. It would be better not to wrap it up, for then the customs officials might ask you to unwrap it, and, if they opened the cover, it would be disastrous.

"On the other hand, it would be well to tie it in careless fashion with a piece of heavy cord, and under that cord you could stuff some folded scientific papers. I think we could slip through that way. You could say, if questioned, that you had nothing to declare, and I could explain that you were an English professor going over to Paris to give a lecture. I believe that would work, for I speak French very fluently, and I am not exactly ugly. A smile from a pretty woman will do wonders with a French customs' officer."

Rymer gazed at her in open admiration.

"I believe you have struck the nail right on the head, Mary," he said. "We will work along those lines. Now, come, my dear girl, we have a lot of work ahead of us to-night. It will take hours to remove the stones from those settings and melt down the metal."

All of which goes to show that the new partnership was progressing most favourably for all concerned.

And Rymer's new partner showed herself quite as valuable in actual deeds as in ideas, for after he had initiated her in the work, her slim, supple fingers worked almost as swiftly as his own. With one brief interval, shortly after midnight, for some light refreshments, they worked, with scarcely a pause, until six o'clock in the morning, when it would have been risky for the girl to remain any longer. There was only a little more to do, and Rymer would be able to complete that before breakfast.

After breakfast Mary Trent was to leave for Horsham with a bag, and shortly after Rymer was to follow. At Croydon they were to join forces again, and from there make their attempt to get the stones across to Paris.

Nor did either of them know that while they worked in the laboratory through the hours of early dawn a crazy-looking apparatus, attached to a small current-testing balloon, was drifting slowly along on a light breeze which was carrying it from London towards Kent.

AS Sexton Blake and Tinker were ushered into Mrs. Stuyvesant Courtlandt's private salon that rather sleepy lady, who met them in a voluminous neglige, never guessed for a single moment that her visitors had just been engaged in what the law terms "burglary and assault." Certainly she read no hint of such a thing in the grave dignity of the elder man, nor in the cheerful countenance of the younger.

"I must apologise for disturbing you at this hour of the night," said Blake. "My only excuse is the knowledge that you would want to be informed at once of anything definite regarding your missing property."

"Quite right, Mr. Blake!" she rejoined crisply. "If you have something definite to tell me, you owe me no apology."

"I have something more than that. I have something to show you. I may be entirely mistaken, and what I have brought may not be part of your property; but I want you to inspect it."

As he spoke, Blake took out the paper packet which had been the proceeds of the burglarious raid he and Tinker had carried out. Crossing to where Mrs. Courtlandt sat, he opened the paper and laid the whole thing in her lap.

She gave a sharp exclamation of delight as she gazed upon the collection of rings, brooches, and other studded ornaments which twinkled up at her. She picked up piece after piece and examined it closely. Finally she spoke.

"You are certainly a quick worker, Mr. Blake," she said happily, her words and accent more pronounced than ever in her excitement. "These are all part of my property. But the larger pieces—the most valuable part of the collection is not here. Where did you find them, and where are the others?"

"I am glad to know that you are able to identify them, Mrs. Courtlandt," he said quietly, with no hint of the relief he felt. "I quite realise that the most valuable portion of the collection is not there, but I have hopes—strong hopes—Mrs. Courtlandt, that I shall be able to trace the other pieces soon, now I want you to lock these away very carefully, and to say nothing absolutely nothing—about receiving

101

them back."

"Why, I will do exactly as you say, Mr. Blake. You have shown that you are handling this case in a most capable way and I shall not do or say a single thing that will place any obstacles in your way. I cannot express how grateful I feel. But can't you tell me a little more?"

"I will tell you as much as I can, Mrs. Courtlandt. These stones which I have returned to you to-night were secured by me and my assistant in a manner which the police would hardly recognise as orthodox. To be quite truthful, we carried out a burglary to-night on mere suspicion. If those rings and other ornaments had not been yours, it would have been necessary for us to return them, for then I should have had no proof that they were other than the perfectly legal property of the man from whom I—er—took them. Do you follow me?"

"I should say I do, Mr. Blake," answered the lady, with sparkling eyes. "And I will tell the world that we haven't got any detectives in New York who can work any quicker than that. Tell me more please."

Blake smiled.

"By to-morrow morning the man from whom I took this portion of your property will be under arrest—on another charge. Two other arrests will, I hope, also be made at an early hour, on a charge which will serve for the time being. I have reason to think that the more valuable part of your property has already passed into the hands of still another individual, and, as that person is the master mind of the whole affair, then you can understand it is very necessary for me to run him to earth before the arrest of the other three becomes known to him. You may rest assured that I shall do everything in my power to find and get possession of the rest of your jewels. That is all I can tell you just now. And, once more, let me impress upon you the necessity for secrecy. I do not want even your man Williams to know what has been done."

"You can trust me completely," .she said quickly.

And that was the second time those exact words had been used within a few hours with reference to the same matter, but with a world of difference in their application.

A few minutes later Blake and Tinker took their departure. As they climbed into the car Tinker gave a prodigious yawn.

"Where now, guv'nor?" he mumbled. "Home?"

Blake paused to light a cigarette before stepping into the car.

"Yes," he said. "I have a little telephoning to do, and then we will turn in. We must be up early. There is a lot ahead of us to-day."

And day it already was, for the sky was now greying in the east.

Once back in the consulting-room, Blake threw aside his coat and seated himself at the desk. Drawing the telephone instrument towards him, he gave a number and waited. Presently he heard a voice, and, after making an inquiry, he had to wait a few minutes before he recognised the well-known tones of Inspector Thomas at the other end of the wire,

"It is Blake speaking, inspector," said Blake, smiling a little at the sleepy irritation displayed by the inspector, "Sorry to wake you up at this hour of the morning, but I have some important information for you."

At once the inspector's voice was keen and crisp.

"What is it, Blake?" he asked quickly.

"I am in possession of some inside information, inspector, which I know to be correct. I think you will want to act on it. To-night a burglary was committed at a bookshop in Old Compton Street. The bookshop is run by a man by the name of Samuels. During the burglary, Samuels himself appeared on the scene, and was assaulted. The burglars escaped, but left him bound and gagged on the floor of his private office, where he still is, unless the policeman on the beat has discovered him. But the curious part of my information is, inspector, that it is not the burglars for whom you should search. On the contrary, the man you will find it expedient—most expedient, inspector—to arrest is Samuels himself!"

"Why, I don't follow you at all, Blake. How do you know about this burglary, and how have you come into possession of so many details?"

"I cannot give you the source of my information," answered Blake, while Tinker, who had guessed what the inspector had said, grinned broadly. "But you can take it from me, that it is correct. Now listen, inspector. I am very serious. This man Samuels is mixed up in the Courtlandt jewels affair. I cannot tell you exactly to what extent yet. But he is in deep enough for you to detain him. But I very strongly recommend you to detain him on some other charge. I leave it to you what that shall be, but I give you my word that you need have no fear of making a mistake. As soon as necessary, I shall place in your hands sufficient proof to justify you. Furthermore, there are two more detentions which I strongly suggest that you make as early as possible. Otherwise, your birds may elude you."

"You have me guessing, Blake. I wish you would tell me just what you mean."

"I will do so all in good time. I can't just yet, Inspector. But, believe me, if you will act on my suggestions you will bring down the biggest game you have tackled for years. You know me well enough to realise that I do not talk moonshine."

"All right, Blake, I will act as you suggest. But for Heaven's sake don't let me down."

"I shall not do that. Now, the other two detentions I want you to make will necessitate your going to Maida Vale. Do you know the Haverdale Mansions there?"

"Of course."

"Very well. If you make investigations, you will find that the man Samuels has a flat there—second floor at number 116a. On that same floor, and directly opposite his flat, is another, at present occupied by two gentlemen who moved in only yesterday, and who as recently as yesterday morning, were staying at the Hotel Venetia. As a matter of fact, they were staying at the Venetia on the night that Mrs. Courtlandt's jewels were stolen."

"What are their names?"

"Thurlow Jordan and Simeon Ferguson."

"What! Are you sure?"

"Perfectly. And, Inspector, let me warn you not to let them slip through your fingers. They are important, most important, as factors in this case. If you will do this, then three of the gaps will be closed. I hope that you will be able to close the remaining gap or gaps very soon."

"Is it any use for me to come to Baker Street?"

"No. Honestly, inspector, I can't tell you any more now, and the least delay is dangerous. Take my advice and act now."

"Right!" said the inspector decisively, "I will."

"Will you telephone me early, say about six, and let me know how you have succeeded?"

"Yes."

With that, Blake hung up, and, after a few minutes conversation with Tinker, they made ready to turn in. But they slept only a few hours. It was just a quarter to six when Brake knocked up Tinker and went along to his bath. He was in the consulting room in a dressing-gown when Inspector Thomas rang up.

"You made no mistake about Samuels," he said grimly. "It was the most complete job I have ever seen. He was bound, gagged, blindfolded, and his ears were stuffed with putty. Something very queer about that. When we released him he was like a crazy man, but that was nothing to the way he went on when he found that he had to come along to the yard. I don't mind telling you, Blake, that he has made all sorts of threats, and if we can't make good on this, it will be good-night for me."

"Don't worry, Inspector. I will place sufficient proof in your hands to put Samuels away for several years. Did you net the other pair?"

"We did—about half an hour ago. They weren't home all night, and rolled up about five o'clock, well primed, I can tell you. We grabbed them before they guessed what was up, and they didn't have a chance to start anything."

"Good work, inspector. Keep them close. By the way, did they have any large amount of money on them?"

"I should say they did—wads of it."

"All Treasury notes? Or some banknotes?"

"Both."

"Here is another tip then, inspector. Take the numbers of those notes. Then find out what bank Samuels uses. See if you can trace any of the notes through his account."

"I will do that. When will I hear from you again?"

"I can't say. I will be as soon as I have something further for you. Good-bye." Blake hung up the receiver and leant back in his chair with a faint sigh of satisfaction.

"So far so good." he muttered. "Now to hear from Stacey; then for Abbey Towers and Professor Andrew Butterfield." He was still in the consulting room taking a cup of tea when the telephone rang again. It proved to be the call from Stacey for which he was waiting.

"I am speaking from Fieldchurch in Kent, Mr. Blake," he said. "I made a landing just outside the village here."

"What luck did you have?"

"Absolutely top-hole. I caught your flare all right, and a little later I picked up the balloon. I had to keep circling pretty low to follow it. I fancy it was a bit overloaded. And then, just about dawn, the light you had arranged went out. But it was light enough to see, and I just kept on in wide circles. Your little plan worked very nicely, for, by actual time it was just four hours and eleven minutes from the time I picked it up until the bag dropped. The balloon shot up very high then, and the last I saw of it, it was drifting towards the sea. I managed a very good landing and found the bag without much difficulty I have just checked up the distance from London. In a straight line it measures off exactly thirty-seven miles. But allowing for vagaries of air currents, I reckon the bag covered nearer forty, and that coincides with the velocity of the wind during those hours. It was quite an interesting test."

"I am extremely obliged to you," said Blake, warmly. "'I had hardly dared hope that it would be successful. What you report is most valuable to me. It confirms in every particular what I wanted to test. Are you off to Croydon now?"

"Yes."

"Well, if you are up in town one day during the week, I wish you would lunch with me. I may be able to tell you the whole story then. I fancy you will find it interesting."

"You can count on me. Good-bye!"

Tinker entered the consulting-room just as Blake hung up the receiver. Blake told him what Stacey had reported, and the lad looked at Blake with undisguised admiration.

"So the dinky little outfit really made good," he exclaimed. "I would have bet that it would have smashed up before it went five miles. And do you really think that is how Mrs. Courtlandt's dressing-case happened to get to the plantation in Lord Ranborough's place, guv'nor?"

"Undoubtedly. Much more scientific means were used, but the principle was the same. Read up that article of which I told you, my lad, and you will see how it was done. Later on I will explain it to you. Now let us get ready for breakfast. I want to start for Abbey Towers early."

An hour later the Grey Panther was speeding along the Horsham Road bound for Abbey Towers, while Professor Andrew Butterfield and his new partner were on their way to Croydon aerodrome.

CHAPTER 11.   The Rush to Paris—Blake's Conclusions—The Meeting With Mary Trent—Some Clever Acting—Collecting up the Loose Threads.

SEXTON BLAKE did not make any attempt at disguise before leaving for Abbey Towers. In the first place, he felt very strongly that he had succeeded in establishing a definite connection between Rymer and the three men whom Inspector Thomas had roped in so quietly.

Blake felt, too, that Rymer's visit to Samuels had had a very definite bearing on the robbery at the Venetia. On reflection, he was of the opinion that, barring the possibility that the rest of the Courtlandt jewels were concealed somewhere about the bookshop premises, Rymer was a very likely custodian.

The swiftness with which Blake had acted the previous night had served to clinch, in more ways than one, the tentative hypothesis he had evolved from the jumble of facts and deductive possibilities, due to the long and careful analysis he had applied to the case.

So far, the chain he was building up had answered every test in a remarkable way, due in no little degree to the boldness with which he had acted on the suggestions arising from the different analyses. He was still at sea as to just how much Rymer had had to do with the actual carrying out of the robbery.

He was inclined to think, after a logical survey of the care Rymer had taken to build up for himself a highly respected position under the name of Professor Butterfield, that he was far too shrewd to commit himself to such an extent that he would place himself beyond the law.

Blake knew the complex nature of the man too well to believe that he would willingly jeopardise that immunity which had been denied him for so many years, and which he had now enjoyed for only a few months. There must have been many, many times when, as he skulked in some far-off corner beyond the rim of the horizon, he must have hungered for England.

On the other hand, Blake also knew to what an extent Rymer would be tempted by the enormous prize represented by the Courtlandt jewels. On that basis Blake was working, and he felt convinced that, even if Rymer had not taken an active part in the robbery, he would, if he could, secure the major part of the booty for himself.

Blake had already ticked off both Jordan and Ferguson as more or less the working tools of a master-mind which had lurked in the background. Samuels he had placed just where he had now proved he belonged—as simply a super-fence in league with the master-crook. If that theory was right, and if his deductions regarding Rymer would hold water, then he knew that he must strike swiftly before the other could break up the balance of the collection.

He knew, too, that if those jewels were in Rymer's possession the time for finesse had passed. It was a case for a bold stroke, and that without delay. If he was on the wrong track, then the worst that could happen would be that Rymer would have the laugh on his side. He would not risk any publicity.

And so it was that as Blake took the wheel of the Grey Panther, he and Tinker were dressed exactly as they would have been for any ordinary motoring journey into the country, excepting that each carried his automatic handy in the side pocket of his coat.

While Blake had taken all possible precautions to keep from publicity any report of the three arrests, he realised that the son of the Jew was an unknown quantity. It had, of course, been impossible to include him in the net that Inspector Thomas had thrown out, and there was not the least evidence to show whether he knew anything of his father's activities or not.

If Rymer should get any report of the arrests before they could reach Abbey Towers, then there was every possibility that he might take to flight. On the other hand, it was equally possible that he would remain to bluff it out. The strongest card in Blake's hand was the fact that, so far, Rymer could hardly know what progress Blake had made, even if he was aware that Blake was working on the case.

And even if he knew that, he could hardly imagine that Blake had him under direct suspicion. For those reasons, Blake thought it quite possible that he would find Rymer at Abbey Towers. He did not know what had transpired there after Rymer's return the previous day.

He mulled the whole thing over in his mind while he drove at a steady pace down through Surrey and into Sussex. He did not approach Abbey Towers by way of Horsham, but took the road through Guildford and on to Godalming, where he cut across the ridge.

This brought him into the Horsham road near Rudgewick, from which small village Abbey Towers was only about two miles distant.

At Rudgewick, Blake made inquiries as to the exact position of the Towers, and, shortly after, he was turning in between the gates.

As he drove between the fine trees, he had to admit that Rymer had certainly succeeded in acquiring a very attractive place, and the fact that a good deal of money had obviously been spent on it, only served to make Blake feel more certain than ever that Rymer would not yield up the security of that retreat without a fight.

Both he and Tinker were attuned for quick action as the Grey Panther came to a stop at the foot of the steps leading to the front entrance. As he had approached, Blake's sharp eyes had noted that a good many of the blinds seemed to be drawn, but thought little of it at the time, as he remembered that Rymer lived alone with probably only a few servants.

Tinker remained in the car while Blake mounted the steps and pressed the bell. After some minutes' wait he heard footsteps on the other side of the door and then the noise of chain and bolts, which struck him as curious, considering that it was just about mid-forenoon. A few moments later the door opened, and Blake found himself confronted by a respectable-looking woman of middle age.

"I understand that Professor Butterfield lives here," said Blake pleasantly. "Can you tell me if he is at home?"

The woman shook her head.

"Professor Butterfield went away this morning," she said.

"Ah! That is most unfortunate. I was anxious to see him on a matter of some importance. Can you tell me if he will return to-day?"

"Oh, no, sir. I do not expect him back for some days. I do not know just when. He said he would telegraph me when he was returning."

Blake had watched the woman's eyes while she was speaking and he felt positive she was speaking the truth.

"You are the housekeeper?"

"Yes, sir."

"It is most important that I should get in touch with the professor," went on Blake. "Do you know where he has gone?"

"No, sir. He didn't say. I asked him about letters and he said keep everything until his return. He drove into Horsham this morning and took the train there. That is all I know, sir,"

Blake thanked her and said he would have to wait until the professor returned. He could do nothing else. It was obvious that the woman knew nothing—that she was a thoroughly respectable soul, who little dreamed that her master was other than the eminent Professor Butterfield. But it showed that something had caused Rymer to clear out very suddenly.

Blake did not believe that it was because he had heard of the arrests. It was practically impossible that he would have done so. It was something else, and Blake made a shrewd guess that the reason was the same that he had feared before—that no time would be lost in splitting up the Courtlandt jewels and camouflaging them among the numerous Russian and Austrian stones that were arriving in Paris, Amsterdam and London.

But where had Rymer gone? That was the puzzle. Had he gone up to London for another interview with Samuels? If that was the case, then, by now, he must know of the latter's arrest. Or had he and Samuels settled all details the previous day, and was Rymer off to carry out a plan already agreed on?

If that were so, then it looked as if he might be headed for the Continent. Was he making for Paris, expecting to meet Samuels there? Or might he be bound for Amsterdam, or some other clearing-place on the Continent? The answer could certainly not be found at Abbey Towers, so, climbing back into the car, Blake turned and headed for Horsham. He stopped there and put through a call to Inspector Thomas at Scotland Yard.

There was an irritating delay while he waited, but at last he heard the inspector's voice. In guarded words Blake told him that he wanted immediate instructions sent out to watch every port for one Professor Andrew Butterfield, giving the inspector a detailed description of what the man looked like.

He did not say that it was Rymer, for that would have helped none, and for personal reasons Blake was not yet ready to disclose everything to the inspector. The inspector promised to send out an urgent call at once instructing the officers at every port to detain the professor if he showed up.

That done, Blake put through another call, this time to Croydon, for he knew it was quite on the cards that Rymer would try and get out of the country by aeroplane. He thought his best plan would be to try and get in touch with Stacey, whom he figured must be back at the aerodrome by now.

In this conjecture he was right, for he found that Stacey had been back nearly an hour. Blake asked him to make inquiries for him, and as soon as he had ascertained whether a Professor Butterfield had either left the aerodrome that morning, or was booked to leave, to telephone through to him at the hotel in Horsham.

Stacey proved himself quite as reliable in this matter as in the difficult test of the night before, for about three quarters of an hour later the call came through. Blake's lips set grimly as he heard what the other had to say.

"Your man left Croydon not an hour ago," said Stacey. "He went in a Blackstone machine to Paris."

"I am very, greatly obliged," said Blake quickly. "Now, I wonder if you would do me another favour. It is essential for me to leave for Paris to-day. I am motoring through from Horsham almost at once. Would you engage two places in one of the machines leaving early in the afternoon, or, if they are all full, will you try and get a special machine for me?"

"Why, of course, with pleasure, Mr. Blake. I will attend to that at once."

Blake thanked him, and hung up. Then he turned to Tinker.

"Come, my lad. We must get to Croydon as quickly as we can. He has gone to Paris."

They hurried out to the car, but, before starting for Croydon, Blake pulled in to the post-office. There he sent a telegram to Mrs. Sophie Courtlandt at the Venetia, that ran as follows:

"Confidential please instruct Williams leave for Paris by air to-day report me on arrival at Carlitz Hotel leaving by air myself.
Sexton Blake."

The girl who took the telegram shot a look of keen interest at Blake as she read the name, and when he asked that the telegram be rushed, she assured him that it would go at once. He thanked her with one of his charming smiles, then rushed back to the car.

It was a wild journey that they had from Horsham to Croydon. Blake let the Grey Panther all out, and, although the road was distinctly bad in places, they covered the distance in a time that would have been quite respectable at Brooklands. At Croydon, Blake went at once to Stacey's office, found that the meteorologist had not been able to get seats for them, but had booked a special machine. He had also very thoughtfully provided a well-filled hamper for the journey.

As the pilot was standing by ready, they wasted very little time, and inside of twenty minutes after reaching Croydon, the 'plane taxied down the field and took off. The 'plane was a speedy twin engine "Crisp," and with perfect flying conditions, as well as a ten-mile visibility, the pilot assured them they would make the journey in something close to record time.

And he did, for, as they circled for the landing at Le Bourget, Blake looked at his watch and found that they had made it in exactly two hours and five minutes— something better than a hundred and twenty miles an hour.

Of course, neither Blake or Tinker had any luggage, for when they had left Baker Street that morning they little dreamed that early afternoon would find them in Paris. But that was a circumstance that did not worry Blake. He knew half a dozen men in Paris whom he could call on for the necessary articles of toilet and for sleeping suits. There was no delay at Le Bourget, and about three-quarters of an hour afterwards they were at the Carlitz.

Blake booked rooms, then had a short interview with the manager, who, of course, knew Blake well, the latter having stayed at the Carlitz often, over a period of many years. He assured Blake that he himself would be delighted to lend him and Tinker all they needed. Then, in the privacy of the sitting-room of their suite, Blake outlined his immediate plans.

"We haven't much to go on, my lad," he said, pacing up and down the room while he talked. "We know that Rymer has come to Paris, and, of course, we must locate him. That is your immediate job. Make a round of all the principal hotels and find out if Professor Butterfield is staying at one of them. We can only surmise what his next move will be. But I am convinced that he has smuggled through with him the missing portion of the Courtlandt jewels, and that is by far the most valuable portion. He won't let any grass grow under his feet in trying to get rid of them. And just there is where we shall have to be sharp. Will he try to make a deal with a 'fence' here, or will he try to get rid of them under cover of other stones?

"If he tries the first way, then we shall have to get in touch with M. Dupuis, the prefect, and get him to throw out a squad to keep a watch on all the known fences. If the latter, then we shall have to work along entirely different lines."

Blake paused, and frowned thoughtfully. "Now, if I were in Rymer's place," he went on slowly, "I think I would adopt the second course. In the first place, we know that Samuels had charge of the least valuable portion of the stones, and, to me, that looks as if his part of the work was to dispose of those through a fence. It would be very risky trying to get rid of the larger pieces in that way. It would need a fence with more than the ordinary command of capital, and more than the ordinary ramifications.

"Even then, he would be nervous of handling them if he guessed that they belonged to the Courtlandt collection. And, of course, so many of those pieces are known in Europe that the stones could not pass through many hands before someone recognised them. A few discreet inquiries, and they would soon discover that the Courtlandt collection had been stolen. We can't expect to keep that secret much longer. Something is bound to leak out.

"No, I believe that Rymer will try the plan of diffusion.

"And I can't imagine a more likely starting-point than the cafe jewel market. If I should prove to be correct in that assumption, then our strongest chance lies in striking first, so to say."

"Just how do you mean, guv'nor?"

"This. Firstly, if Rymer tries to dispose of the stones in that way, he must first start the word going cautiously that he has the stones to sell. Then some of the dealers in that market will prick up their ears and keep their eyes open for likely buyers. All right. But if I can get to the cafe jewel market before Rymer strikes it, and drop a word in the right quarter, hinting that I know a man who is in the market to buy on a very large scale, then there is a chance that Rymer may be steered to that man.

"Moreover, if I can only get there first, he will not be suspicious, for he will not dream that I am in Paris and on his trail. It is worth trying, and while you are scouting about the hotels, I will see what I can do. If old Acier is still active in the cafe market, I might be able to make use of him. He hasn't forgotten that I saved him a considerable amount of money at one time. If that fails, then we shall have to try direct action. Now, my lad, off with you!"

Tinker departed hot foot, and, a few moments later, Blake followed. He secured a taxi outside the hotel, and instructed the driver to go to Montmartre. He had the man draw up some distance from the cafe which was his objective, and made his way along on foot towards the little place that is, perhaps, one of the strangest jewel markets in the whole world. He little guessed that the plan he was putting into effect was to bring him one of the biggest surprises he had ever experienced.

Nothing is definitely known as to origin of the queer little cafe jewel market in Montmartre. Possibly it had its beginning in the same romantic way in which Lloyds developed from the gatherings of a few men in that ancient London coffee-house. Be that as it may, the jewel market has not moved to more commodious premises, but still carries on in the same little rendezvous, where, in a single market, rubies and diamonds, sapphires and pearls worth fabulous sums are passed from hand to hand in small bits of tissue paper as carelessly as a grocer would handle lumps of sugar.

It is a quaint little place that cafe, and in keeping with its character are the dealers who frequent it. The casual visitor to Paris would find it difficult to believe that these nondescript men, some of them dressed worse than shabbily, were trading, by means of a single word or a nod, in gems of such value.

On busy days the tables overflow even on to the pavement, and, once started on its round of inspection, a paper of gems may pass through two score hands before finding its way back to its owner. And yet back it comes, just as it left, not a stone missing, for in that market the slightest attempt at trickery would mean instant expulsion from that exclusive group—a big price to pay, and one that would mean commercial ruin.

And those men there formed, too, the whole barometer of the jewel market. They knew every famous stone in Europe, and a good many in America, from personal examination. Through some one of that group practically every jewel sold in Paris must pass at some time or other, and that was why Sexton Blake was bound there.

If Huxton Rymer tried to dispose of any of the Courtlandt collection in Paris, it was almost a certainty that one of those men or an associate would be invited to act as a medium.

The dealing was in full swing when Blake arrived. From the tables on the terrace he concluded it was a busy session, and as he gazed into the crowded interior of the cafe he saw that this was so.

The particular man he sought was a dealer in only a small way, but Blake knew that he was one of the shrewdest men in the trade in Paris, and dead straight. He had done more than one favour in the past for old Acier, and he thought, if he could lay his trap through the innocent participation of the dealer, Rymer might rise to the bait.

It was difficult to make his way through the press of tables inside, and, moreover, he was looked upon frowningly by those who knew him only as a stranger. But Blake persisted, with a good-humoured smile, and presently had the satisfaction of seeing the man he sought. He was sitting in one corner, near a door that Blake knew led to a small room beyond.

He did not see the detective until Blake was close beside him. Then he looked up, but as his lips were about to form Blake's name the latter shook his head. At another gesture from Blake, he rose, and they passed through the door to the other room. There they shook hands.

"I am sorry to have disturbed you, M. Acier," said. Blake. "I came here, however, to see you particularly. Briefly, I want you to do something for me."

"I am delighted to see you. M. Blake! And you want me to do something for you? I shall be glad to. Pray tell me what it is!"

Blake proceeded to do so, and for five minutes spoke rapidly in low tones. He did not explain why he wanted the dealer to disseminate certain information among the others, but when he had finished it had been arranged as he desired. He knew that inside half an hour every dealer in the place would know that M. Acier had a prospective purchaser for exceptionally choice stones on a very large scale.

That would put every man on the qui vive, and it must follow that if any dealer was offered stones of that description he would at once get in touch with M. Acier. Which was exactly what Blake desired. The dealer invited him to take a cordial, but, remembering that, if his theory was correct, Rymer might turn up at any time, he refused, as he had no wish to be seen there by the adventurer.

And, indeed, less than a minute later he had reason to commend his own caution, for, even as he opened the door to pass into the cafe, he saw Rymer himself standing out on the pavement, gazing into the cafe, as though he intended entering.

Blake whispered a word to M. Acier, and pushed him over the threshold. He was sure Rymer had not yet seen him, for the interior of the cafe was gloomy, and the back was considerably obscured by the clouds of smoke which rose from two score pipes and cigarettes.

Blake closed the door after the dealer, then, seeing another door on the opposite side of the room, he crossed and opened it. It led into a corridor, and, following it along, Blake found that the door at the end led to the other side of the cafe. He passed out there, and, once in the street, took the first turning to the right.

It is not surprising that Blake was filled with a feeling of deep satisfaction as he made his way down the hill towards the Boulevard Montmatre. He had formed a theory, and had acted on it boldly. He knew now that his reasoning had been right, and only the swiftness with which he had acted had enabled him to lay his trap before Rymer arrived at the jewel market.

It was, on the face of it, an extraordinary thing that Rymer had acted just as Blake had anticipated, but, in reality, it was not very wonderful considering the long years the detective had spent in studying the idiosyncrasies of the criminal mind. Many of his successes had been due to nothing else than his capacity for thinking as the criminal would think, and acting as the criminal would act, under certain given circumstances.

And on this particular occasion it had been a strong card that Rymer had no suspicion that Blake was so close on his heels.

Once free of the quarter, Blake hailed a taxi and drove straight back to the Carlitz. On his arrival there he found that Williams, Mrs. Courtlandt's courier, had arrived. Blake secured a room for him adjoining his bedroom; then, while he awaited Tinker's return, he detailed his plans to the American.

Blake's original purpose in requesting Mrs. Courtlandt to send Williams across to Paris was because he wanted close at hand someone who knew positively each stone in the Courtlandt collection, and, of course, Williams, in whose care they had been on many occasions, would have that knowledge. Of course, when Blake sent the telegram from Horsham he had not fully formulated the plan which he now hoped to carry through, providing Rymer rose to the fly he had so carefully cast.

Rymer might not do so, but there was always a chance, and Blake was determined to be ready for him if he should do so. Hence the pains he took to secure a room for Williams adjoining his own.

"Now, this is what I propose," he said, when he had informed the astonished American that some of the stones had already been recovered in London and handed to Mrs. Courtlandt. "I have reason to believe that the balance of the collection has been smuggled across to Paris. Whether any attempt has been made yet to remove the stones from the mountings I do not know, but I am inclined to think that this will be done before the stones are offered for sale. As I have already explained, we have gathered in three of the persons concerned in this robbery, and I am in possession of sufficient evidence to convict all three.

"On the other hand, the man who is still at large, and who, I fear, has so guarded himself that we shall find it difficult to bring anything home to him, unless we find him in actual possession of the jewels, is the master-brain of the whole affair. He is one of the shrewdest and most daring criminal adventurers I have ever come across, and I speak from knowledge, for I have met him many times."

"You know him, then?"

"Yes."

"Do you mind telling me who he is?"

"Have you ever heard of Dr. Huxton Rymer?"

"Good heavens! I have heard a lot about him. Is he the man?"

"He is. And now you know why we must bait our trap very skillfully if we are to catch him."

"Exactly. What do you propose, Mr. Blake?"

"I have done all I can to entice him here with the stones. If what I have planned works, then there is a possibility that he may put in an appearance to-morrow. If he does not, then we must try something else. But if he does come, then your part in the affair is to pose here as a wealthy American who wishes to buy stones of exceptional value and in large quantities. You will receive your visitors in this room. It may be that several people may call—ordinary dealers, and, possibly, people having brought stones through from Russia or Austria, for the rumour that I have started is already being circulated among all the dealers in Paris. However, in each case but the one in which we are interested it will not be difficult for you to temporise.

"In the meantime, I shall be close at hand in the adjoining room here, which happens to be my bedroom. We shall keep the communicating door unlocked, and beneath the carpet I propose running a bit of wire, which will end in a button in this room. That button will be underneath the carpet directly beneath the table at which you will be sitting. In my room it will communicate with a small buzzer. Then if any of your visitors offers you stones which you recognise as belonging to the Courtlandt collection, you will at once press the button. The rest will be my work. Do you follow?"

"Perfectly. The plan sounds good to me, Mr. Blake. If our bird shows up, I guess we ought to be able to sprinkle a little salt on his tail."

"We will not be too confident, but if Rymer enters this room he won't go out until I give the word," said Blake grimly.

They were still discussing their plans when Tinker showed up. He greeted Williams, then turned to Blake.

"No luck, guv'nor. I couldn't locate him anywhere."

"Never mind," rejoined Blake. "He has probably thought it advisable to go to one of the smaller hotels. We may pick him up yet."

"How did you make out?" asked Tinker.

Blake told him what he had done and how he had caught a glimpse of Rymer at the cafe jewel market. Tinker was jubilant, and inclined to think that the circumstances augured well for the success of Blake's plans.

"Don't crow until we have trapped our bird," advised Blake drily. Then he gave Tinker detailed instructions as to the things he wished him to procure in order that he could arrange the button and buzzer. Tinker went off to see if he could find a shop still open, while Blake and Williams devoted another half-hour to the details of the plan.

After dinner that evening, Blake arranged his battery and wire, and placed the table in Williams's room just over the little bulge in the carpet where the button had been placed. None of them left the hotel, for Blake thought it wiser to be on hand in case M. Acier should telephone or call. But no word came, and it was in a very uncertain frame of mind that Blake finally retired.

Early the next morning, Williams, after a hurried breakfast, took up his place in his room after leaving word in the office that in case anyone asked for him he would be there all the morning. Before ten o'clock came, it was evident that M. Acier had not lost any time, for the first sign came with an inquiry for M. Williams from an elderly lady, who was accompanied by her daughter.

They were shown up to Williams's room, and, while the interview was in progress, Blake and Tinker were esconced in Blake's bedroom, awaiting the result. But no ring came from Williams, and when Blake heard the door of the other room close he entered. Williams shook his head.

"It was a Russian countess and her daughter," he said. "She had some fine stones, which she said she had managed to bring with her when she fled from Russia. But she was on the level, all right. There were none of the Courtlandt stones among them."

At that moment the faint whirr of the telephone in Blake's sitting-room came to them. Blake hurried through his bedroom to the instrument. Taking down the receiver he heard the tones of M. Acier at the other end of the wire.

"M. Blake, I have news for you," he said. "I have just heard from a colleague, M. Landelle, that he has been approached with the offer of some very fine stones. I have arranged to meet him in a few minutes. He is bringing his client with him. I have told him that if the sale goes through my client he will receive the commission just the same. Is that satisfactory, M. Blake?"

"Perfectly, M. Acier. Have you any idea of the identity of the client?"

"No; I have not discovered that yet. Shall I bring him on there?"

"If you will, please. The gentleman here, who is interested, is now in his room and can be seen at once. Shall I tell him that he may expect you?"

"Yes. We shall be there within half an hour."

Blake hung up the receiver and returned to Williams's room.

"My dealer is bringing a client," he announced. "He has got in touch through another dealer. M. Acier doesn't know who the client is. But they will be here inside half an hour. It may be our bird or it may not. In any event, be on your guard, Williams."

Blake and Tinker then returned to Blake's bedroom and closed the door. They chatted in low tones until they heard a door close and then came sounds of voices in the next room. At that moment the telephone again rang in Blake's bedroom, and with a frown of annoyance, he motioned for Tinker to go and answer it. The lad was still speaking to someone when suddenly the little buzzer at Blake's feet whirred.

With a smothered exclamation Blake straightened up. He touched the side pocket of his coat, where his automatic lay, then he strode to the communicating door. He laid his fingers on the knob, then he jerked the door open and stepped through, ready to face the one man he wanted to see just then more than anyone else. But as he paused his eyes widened in amazement. Instead of Dr. Huxton Rymer, Blake found himself gazing into a pair of very pretty eyes—the eyes of a very self-possessed young woman.

His mind worked swiftly. Had Williams pressed the button by mistake? His glance went to the American, who nodded. And just then Tinker returned, to pause and gaze past Blake in amazement. Whatever the explanation might be, it was plain that the young woman, who stood facing Williams across the table, had offered some of the Courtlandt jewels, which he had recognised. And that was enough for Blake to stride forward.

He paused by the table and gazed down at the great heap of gems, which lay outspread on the green pad which Williams had arranged on the table. One glance told him that not a few of the jewels were there, but that the whole of the missing portion must lie before his eyes. Then his eyes went again to the girl. He was puzzled—as a matter of fact, at that moment Blake was completely at sea.

He had entered that room fully expecting to find Dr. Huxton Rymer there, accompanied by M. Acier and the other dealer. Instead, he found a young and pretty girl— alone. He found out later, that the message Tinker had taken on the telephone had been from M. Acier in the hotel office to inform Blake that the client had insisted on going up alone.

And yet, instinctively, Blake knew that the self-possessed young woman before him must have got those stones from Rymer. Was her possession of them an innocent one? It hardly seemed likely. Blake gestured towards the heap of gems.

"Do you mind telling me where you got these jewels?" he asked in French.

The girl's brows lifted.

"I do not know by what right you ask, monsieur; I understood that my business was with this gentleman here. It seems you have made a rude intrusion. I do not like this sort of thing. I will take my jewels elsewhere."

With that she made a movement to pick up the heap of gems, but Blake's hand shot out and covered them.

"Not yet, mademoiselle," he said softly, "If my intrusion appeared rude, I am quite ready to ask your pardon. Nevertheless, you must answer my question."

"Indeed. And may I ask why, monsieur?"

"You may. These jewels are stolen property. Therefore, mademoiselle, I think you will see the wisdom of telling me how they came into your possession."

She gazed at him without the flicker of an eyelash.

"Stolen property," she said coolly. "Oh, no, monsieur. That is impossible. They are my property, brought by me from Russia."

"Are you, then, a Russian refugee?" asked Blake quickly, speaking in Russian.

The girl gazed at him uncomprehendingly. Blake laughed.

"You brought them from Russia, and yet you do not understand Russian," he said. "That won't wash, mademoiselle. These stones are, as I have said, stolen property. Your evasion just now proves that you know that as well as I. It proves, too, that you received them from a gentleman who calls himself Professor Andrew Butterfield. Now will you answer my question or must I take other measures to make you speak?"

The girl stared at Blake in silence for some moments. Then her lips opened and she whispered hoarsely.

"Stolen! Is this true? I know I evaded the truth when I said they had been brought from Russia. I had been told to say that. But—stolen? Are you sure, monsieur?"

"Absolutely, mademoiselle," said Blake, speaking more gently.

Her hand went to her head.

"Stolen," she whispered again. "How—oh, what shall I do? I—I—" Then her eyes closed, and she staggered against the desk. She would have fallen had not Blake caught her. As it was, she slipped through his arms loosely.

"She has fainted," said Blake curtly. "Get that flask out of my room, Tinker."

As he spoke he carried the inanimate form across and laid it on the couch. Williams had jumped up, and was filling a glass with water. As her head touched the pillow her eyelids fluttered open, and Blake bent to hear the whispered words that came from between her lips.

"Air—air," she was saying, so Blake jumped up and crossed to the window to open it. He was just raising the sash when a sharp exclamation from Williams caused him to turn round. And then he stood absolutely paralysed for the moment at what he saw.

The girl, who, a moment before, had been apparently in a dead faint, was now on her feet. She was already half-way to the door, and in her hand was a small automatic with which she was covering both

Blake and Williams. The American looked utterly foolish as he stood by the washstand holding a glass of water in one hand while he gaped at the girl.

"Just as you are," she said coolly. "One little move, and I fire."

Another backward step and she reached the door. Her fingers fumbled at the key, and then Blake dived. The pistol cracked once, then Blake came to his feet and sprang for the door. But ere he managed to reach it, it had been slammed, and, even as he tugged at the handle, he heard the key turn. Then came a low silvery laugh, and the faint sound of pattering footsteps along the hall.

Blake gave a savage exclamation, and turning, dashed into his own room, colliding with Tinker as he did so.

"Come on," he called, and with Tinker and Williams at his heels, went through his room like a cyclone and dashed along the corridor. Through the glass doors of the lift he could see the wire moving. That was sufficient to tell him that the girl had already managed to get that much start. Blake turned and led the way down the back staircase, taking them three steps at a time.

As they reached the lobby people stared in amazement at the three flying figures who tore past and headed for the door. A stupid porter, thinking that they might be thieves, barred their way, causing the loss of a precious half-minute before Blake could hurl him aside. Then he reached the commissionaire.

"Young woman just went out," he panted. "Blue suit, black hat with a red feather in it. Did you see her?"

"Why, yes, sir, There was a car waiting for her. Gentleman with a beard was in it. They drove off only a minute ago," Blake's eyes followed the course of the street, wondering which unit among all that traffic might contain the fugitives. For that the bearded man had been Rymer, he did not doubt, But now he knew that the girl had told her story, and that the pair would be already in flight. He shrugged his shoulders and re-entered the lobby. As he did so, M. Acier and another man approached him.

"What is it? What has happened?" asked the dealer excitedly.

"Come upstairs and I will explain," answered Blake.

With that he led the way back to Williams' room, where he told the astonished dealers what had happened. Then he submitted the gems to M. Acier for his opinion, and, after a careful examination, the expert picked out several large stones which he knew had belonged to the Courtlandt collection.

"There is no doubt," he said. "But we have heard nothing about the Courtlandt jewels being stolen."

"I know. We kept it quiet," answered Blake. "We got back some of the stones in London and, I fancy, this lot will practically complete the collection."

"But it is amazing!" exclaimed the other dealer. "I had no idea of this! To think that that young lady was trying to dispose of such property. What will you do, Monsieur?"

That was the question that Tinker and Williams also wanted to ask. Blake only shrugged.

"Nothing at present," he said. "It is not pleasant to realise that we were all so completely fooled by a girl, but there it is. However, we have recovered the stones, and that is the chief thing. I shall report to my client in London, and, if she wishes to make further efforts to track down the fugitives, why, I suppose, I shall try and do so. But for the present I shall let things rest as they are. As for you and your colleague, M. Acier, I may say that there is a very large reward for the recovery of these stones, and you will both share in it. I will communicate with you later on after my return to London."

The two dealers thanked him, and, after a few more words, withdrew. When they had gone, Blake took out a cigar and bit on it savagely. Then, suddenly, his eyes fell on the tumbler which Williams had dropped to the floor, and he began to laugh softly.

"I think we must confess that the joke is on us," he said with returning good humour, "That girl was one of the most consummate actresses I have ever met. I would have wagered any sum that it was a perfectly genuine swoon. Williams, if I may say so without offence, you looked silly with that glass of water in your hand."

The American grinned sheepishly, and Tinker chuckled.

"I wonder who she is?" said the lad. "When she was cornered here and got away with that bluff, it was like the way Mademoiselle Yvonne used to wriggle out of a tight corner."

Blake smiled reminiscently; then he pointed towards the heap of gems.

"Better lock those up, Williams. We will have Mrs. Courtlandt check them up when we get back to London. I am afraid she will never recover the settings, but she won't mind that much, as long as she gets the stones back."

"She won't think of the settings," grunted Williams. "And I'll tell the world, Mr. Blake, that you are sure some swift worker. I don't know how you have managed to do what you have done so quickly. I'll bet that stout gentleman from Scotland Yard is still chasing his own shadow."

Blake laughed as he thought of how anxiously Inspector Thomas was waiting for the promised evidence that would justify the three arrests he had made. Then he glanced at his watch.

"We will try to get a 'plane back early this afternoon," he announced. "See what you can arrange, Tinker."

They left the hotel soon after lunch, and were back in London by tea-time. While Williams went on to the Venetia to hand over the gems to Mrs. Courtlandt. Blake and Tinker drove to Scotland Yard to see Inspector Thomas. Then, in the inspector's office, Blake gave that official a detailed review of the whole case, beginning from the moment when he had begun to puzzle over the bit of green cord that had been tied to the handle of the dressing case, and tracing his deductions along, step by step, until the trail had at last led him to Dr. Huxton Rymer.

As he spoke of the test they had made with the balloon, of the burglary he and Tinker had committed, and of the patience with which he had picked up each loose thread and gradually untangled it, the inspector gazed at him almost unbelievingly. At last, when Blake had finished, he said:

"Well, Blake, I certainly take off my hat to you, particularly over that bit of green cord, and the way you figured out how the dressing-case must have come in the plantation on Lord Ranborough's place. But about Rymer—I think it is about time we threw the net out for him."

Blake shrugged. "I don't think you will have much success, inspector. If I am any judge of Rymer, he is probably out of France by now. And you can take it from me that he won't be hampered by the fact that the girl of whom I told you is with him. They may have parted and taken different routes. But she is as sharp as a needle. You might keep an eye on Abbey Towers, however. One of them may, eventually, try and work back there to get things they need."

The inspector made a note of this, but though he kept a close watch on the Towers for many weeks, he never got a single clue to the whereabouts of either Rymer or his mysterious partner. As for Mrs.

Courtlandt, she was so happy over the return of the jewels—not one was missing—that she didn't give a thought to the settings, remarking to Blake that it was time, anyway, that they should be reset. She was more than generous in the matter of the reward, and the warm-hearted woman quite embarrassed Blake by the vehemence of her gratitude.

As a case, it certainly had revealed Sexton Blake in one of his most brilliant veins, even, though, in his own mind, his success lacked something by the fact that, through the ingenuity of a slip of a girl, Rymer had managed to elude him. But he knew, too, that a day would come, and for that day he would be ready. So, with that reflection, he turned his attention to other pressing matters.

THE END.
[50100 WORDS]

THE END.

The Affair of the Wandering Musician.

By Anon.

A Grand, Complete Story.

Relating one of Sexton Blake's Earliest Cases.

IN the very large circle of Sexton Blake's acquaintances there were some for whom, in spite of sundry failings he had quite a special regard. And within this more exclusive list he would certainly have written the name of Barry Luton.

Luton was a delightful fellow, with an unfailing ability for getting into awkward scrapes that was slightly counterbalanced by considerable adroitness in getting out of them, coupled with an unflagging hopefulness of disposition. He had followed a dozen professions, and, without being a conspicuous failure in any, had always turned impatiently to something fresh before his genuine abilities had had time to carry him on to success.

Blake, returning early one Sunday evening from an idle stroll in the park, found Luton ensconced in a chair near the fireplace. The visitor sprang to his feet at the sound of footsteps, and Blake realised at once that his friend was in a state of acute distress. His face was tense and drawn, his eyes heavy, and his clothing looked as if it had been slept in. There was nothing but sheer, desperate relief in the fervour with which he grasped Blake s hand.

"What's wrong?" said the latter immediately, seeing that every moment which delayed Barry's explanation was clearly adding to his nervous misery. "Too many bills? Too many brandies-and-sodas?"

"Don't joke," said Barry harshly, "or I shall make a fool of myself! The simple fact is that I'm involved in an affair that, without landing me in the police-courts, has driven me to the verge of suicide, though Heaven knows that I meant no harm when I embarked upon it!"

"Then take a cigar, and give me the facts as soon as you can."

Barry threw himself back in a chair, and selected a cigar with fingers which he tried to keep from shaking.

"Then here's for the truth," he said. "It all dates from three days ago. I'd been out of a berth for a month or so, and my usual luck in getting another seemed to have deserted me, for at every single place I tried they seemed to be full up to overflowing, I was even driven to running a couple of agencies, but no one seemed keen enough on

126

sewing-machines or books to make the game worth while, and the mistresses were insolent, and the maids familiar, at most of the houses where I called. An article I sent to "The Imperial Magazine" brought me in a couple of guineas, and that reminded me that the editor had once been rather a pal of my father's. I called on him, and the upshot was that he offered to take a series of articles on London life, at the usual rates, if I could strike something sufficiently original.

"It was this last word which was really at the bottom of the whole business. For, during my wanderings, I'd had occasion to pass down a street near my diggings a good many times, and had time to notice one rather curious incident connected with it. The street itself—Latymer Grove, Bloomsbury—is as straight and gloomy a thoroughfare as one could find in London, with rows of dun-coloured houses, mostly occupied with people who let lodgings of the two-guineas-a-week class. And between ten in the morning and six at night, when all the young men inhabitants are in the City, the place is about as lively as the Sahara Desert.

"One man, however, appeared to find it satisfactory enough, and he was a disreputable-looking foreigner who used to come regularly, wet or fine, playing a miserable tune, which I only heard him vary once, upon a penny whistle. He would walk slowly from one end of the road to the other, and though I don't think I ever saw the passers-by give him anything, the fact didn't appear to depress him in the least. Generally before leaving he would call at one of the houses—No. 11—and return from the back-door with a bagful of broken victuals.

"I caught sight of the owner of the house once or twice. He is a stout little fellow, with a hooky nose and a slightly-lame leg. He's probably an Italian also, but it struck me several times that the gentleman with the whistle was trading a trifle too much on the fact. He visited the street a bit too often in the end, for the police hauled him up—I happened to be interested in a case in the court at the time—on a charge of begging. He protested his innocence in execrable English, but they fined him ten shillings, upon hearing which Hooky-nose came forward from the back of the court, and, as the prisoner didn't appear to have sixpence, paid up like a gentleman.

"A few days later the very same thing was repeated. Pietro—I think he gave that as his first name—again had an interview with the magistrates, gibbered and waved his hands for about ten minutes, and was again saved by his friend. The whole affair struck me as being rather odd, and when it was enacted for the third time, I decided that the first of my series of articles was ready to hand.

"No doubt I acted like a fool, no doubt I shall go on doing so to the end of the chapter; but there was a spice of adventure about the thing which lured me on. And what I did was not very desperate, after all. I merely waited until a particularly dark and gloomy morning, rigged myself up in the shabbiest clothes I possessed, and pressing on an old bowler-hat—the very spit of Pietro's!—down over my forehead, sneaked out an hour before the usual serenading on the penny whistle commenced, and with one of my own, began playing the second air I'd once heard Pietro indulge in, and which happened to be an odd little tune that had stuck in my memory.

"The things that one anticipates never come off, and so far as having anything to record for the benefit of the 'Imperial Magazine' went, I might as well have stopped at home. Not a soul from one end of the street to the other, took the smallest interest in either me or my whistle, and there wasn't even a policeman in sight to arrest me for begging.

"However, to round off the entertainment I played for about five minutes opposite No. 11, and then wandered round to the back door for the usual donation. Again it was evident that my luck was out, for in spite of repeated knockings, no one came, and on peering in, I came to the conclusion that there was nobody in the house.

"I left at last, fairly disgusted, and prepared to go home. But before I'd gone a dozen yards I came face to face with friend Pietro. And, upon my word, Blake, in the general gloom and darkness, we were as alike as two peas!

"To tell the truth, I had clean forgotten him, but in any case it seemed to be merely a matter for some small compensation for poaching on his preserves. But before I could get in a word of explanation, he literally flung himself upon me, snatched the whistle out of my hands, and broke out in a stream of prayers, curses, and general vituperation in a mixture of Italian and English. I tried to get in a sentence or so edgeways, and—like the ignorant fool that I was— even offered him money. And all the time he was waving his arms and screaming, in a perfect frenzy of rage and terror, that nothing on earth could save him now, and that he was a dead man. 'You keel me!' he said, over and over again, and 'You die, too, when they know!'

"The whole thing was so absurd that, although perhaps a little impressed at the time, I was inclined to attribute his excitement to temperament, rather than the fact that there was any serious danger. I left him still storming, and went home with a vague idea of using the incident for some article or story. I was wet through and tired, and pretty well at the end of my tether, and I spent the rest of the day wondering whether I should spend the next in the workhouse infirmary with rheumatic fever.

"In the afternoon my landlady, who's a good sort, brought up one of the late editions of an evening paper to cheer me up a bit. And there, in the stop-press column, I found this"—Luton produced a cutting from his pocket, and handed it to Blake— "and realised that Pietro's fears had some justification, after all! It's in the Sunday papers, of course, and you may have read the account."

"I didn't come back to town until late last night," said Blake, "and I don't generally see the weekly periodicals."

He took the cutting from Luton's still shaking hand, and read;

"A ghastly discovery was made by a constable this afternoon in Latymer Grove, West, when, on glancing into the area of an unoccupied house which stands at the corner, he perceived the body of a man lying dead, with a small, curioussly shaped wound in the breast, and the letters 'M.N.' scrawled in charcoal on his cheek. The man, who was subsequently reported to be a begging musician, known locally as 'Pietro,' has since been removed to the mortuary for formal identification."

"He was right, poor beggar, as you see," Parry continued gloomily. "But that isn't all. For by the last post yesterday I received this."

He drew from his pocket a postcard, and laid it on the table. It was addressed to himself, and on the other side bore simply the rough outline of a hand, drawn in charcoal, beneath which were the same letters .which had disfigured the dead man's face.

Blake's expression changed as he looked at it.

"Woman's writing—posted at 3.30 p.m. at Westminster."

"Yes. What does it mean?" asked Barry, in a high-pitched, hysterical voice. "It can't be a practical joke, and, so far as I am aware, I haven't an enemy in the world."

"It certainly isn't a joke," said Blake, very gravely. "In fact, to be quite candid, I think you have blundered into serious danger. If you would care to spend the night here I can put you up a bed."

Barry, for all that he was no coward paled a little.

"Do you mean that it is as serious as that?"

"At any rate, I think it would he advisable for you to stay where you are for the present. In fact, don't leave the house, under any circumstances whatever, until I get back, even though you get a message from me asking you to."

Barry stared blankly at his friend, who was struggling into a long, grey ulster.

"Then where are you going?" he asked.

"Oh, merely out on business! I may not be back to-night, but I'll tell the housekeeper to look after you properly. Goodbye!"

And Blake, with a cheerful nod to his guest had descended the stairs before Barry had had time to recover from his amazement.

Half an hour later the latter was aroused from an uneasy doze by Mrs. Bardell opening the door, her face indicative of genuine distress.

"There's a man below with a message for you, sir."

"For me?" Barry sprang to his feet.

"Yes, sir. Mr. Blake has been very badly hurt by a taxicab, and has been taken to St. Stephen's Hospital. There's an urgent message from him asking you to come at once."

Barry made an instinctive dash for his coat and hat.

"Is the injury very serious, then?"

"They're afraid that one of the ribs has torn the lung, sir."

Barry was already at the door, when, to her everlasting amazement, he suddenly tore off his coat and hat, and flung them on the table again.

"I can't go! Tell the man it's out of the question!"

"Sir!"

"Explain that I've another engagement anything you like!"

For the memory of Blake's final request had suddenly leapt into his brain. And as Mrs. Bardell, shocked and distressed, withdrew, Barry flung himself back into the chair again.

"I wish to Heaven he'd never left the house!" he said.

  * * * *

In the meantime, Blake, unscathed by taxicabs or any other danger, had been going quietly and steadily about the business in hand. His first act had been to drive to the mortuary to which the wretched, shabbily-dressed victim had been carried. He had no difficulty in obtaining permission to view the body, upon which, however, no papers or articles had been found that could throw any further light upon the tragedy.

Blake made a minute examination through a pocket-lens of the small punctured wound in the breast. Then, no vehicle being handy, he walked past his own door to Latymer Grove, and spent a few minutes in conversation with the constable on duty, at the corner. The man, like many of his brother officers in London, knew him, and eventually accompanied him to the house at No. 11.

There, after a little skilful manoevering, Blake succeeded in effecting an entrance by way of the scullery window, and the two men began a dreary pilgrimage from one deserted room to another. They were simply those of an ordinary middle-class villa, the furniture being old-fashioned, but in good order, and the whole interior indicative of the probable early return of the owner.

Blake ranging the hall, caught sight of a couple of excessively rusty military trophies hanging upon the wall. He mounted a chair, took down and examined them, and climbed down again with a little grunt of satisfaction. From the hall he wandered into the bed-rooms, and in one of these he picked up a crumpled and discarded luggage-label, which he slipped into his pocket. And it was from the dusty obscurity of the space between the rafters and the roof that the constable waiting below next heard Blake's voice.

"I don't think there's any reason for my staying longer, Carroll," he said; "and, by skirting a few chimney-stacks and crossing a couple of roofs, I find that I shall be able to descend without much difficulty by the stables at the end. But before I go, I want to give you one or two important instructions."

"Yes sir" said P.-c. Carroll, with an intelligent nod. He had known Blake too long to be astonished if he had announced his intention of departing by airship.

"You will keep this house under close observation for the rest of the day, and arrest and detain in custody any person of either sex who may enter, or attempt to enter, during that time. I am going to call on Inspector Coutts, who is a personal friend of mine, later on, and will explain the circumstances to him."

"Yes, sir," said the constable again, and immediately proceeded to let himself out of the building, which, as he afterwards confessed, "gave him 'orrid creeps."

Blake, emerging eventually in the stable-yard—whose owner, at the sight of a ten-shilling note, abandoned the indignation he had hastily assumed—climbed into a passing taxi, and drove with all possible speed to Waterloo Station. And there—alert decisive, and not to be deflected from his purpose by unwilling officials—he at length obtained the information he sought, and in the lengthening hours of that Sunday evening emerged again with a look on his face that prepared the cabman for the fare he received.

"As hard as you can go to Scotland Yard, and from there to 3, Messenger Square, when I'm ready!" Blake said.

It was nearly an hour later when Barry staring moodily at the blazing coals, heard the clatter of hoofs on the asphalt outside, and from the window saw, with a vast sense of relief, the figures of Blake and another man emerge from a vehicle. There was the sound of a key turning in the lock, and of double footsteps mounting the stairs. The door opened, and then for once the over-wrought nerves of Barry Luton played him false, and in the presence of his friend, standing triumphant and uninjured, but very weary, at his side, he dropped his head upon the table, and broke into foolish, boyish weeping.

"I—I'm sorry," he said, looking up with a flushed face a moment, later. "But, after receiving a message that you'd been pretty well done for in an accident—"

"H'm! I expected as much," said Blake, with a coolness which, as it was intended, did more to pull his visitor together than the decoction he was mixing from the contents of syphon and tantalus. "And the fact that you ignored it has, without any doubt whatever, been the means of saving your life."

"What has happened?" Barry asked, when the introduction to Inspector Coutts had been duly made. He glanced nervously, and still somewhat shamefaced, from one man to the other.

"Oh, I fancy we shall get the fellows who were responsible for Pietro's murder right enough!"

"Then there was more than one concerned in it?"

"In all probability three."

Coutts, who had been standing, quietly near, interrupted:

"You've told me something of Mr. Luton's connection with this ghastly affair," he said, "but not all the steps which led to your calling at Scotland Yard to-night. And since we both appear to be in ignorance—"

Blake settled himself back in his favourite chair.

"As I hinted to Barry, he had blundered into an infinitely more serious thing than he imagined. I strongly suspected, almost from the first, that Pietro was not merely the street-beggar he seemed, and that some intimate connection between the gentleman at No. 11 and himself was the chief reason for his remarkably regular visits to Latymer Grove.

"My theory crystallised into a certainty when I heard that he had been befriended no less than three times in succession at the police-court by Tutelli, as the name of the occupier of the house is given in the directory. And when you"—Blake nodded at Barry— "appeared on the scene, and, by merely playing that alternative tune of Pietro's, flung the man into such a frenzy of terror and agitation, it was also evident that the melody itself had some especial significance; that, in fact, it served to convey either that all was well, or the reverse, to the occupants of No. 11.

"You unconsciously played the tune which constituted a warning, and from the state of the attic, it is pretty evident that Tutelli and the woman who afterwards wrote the postcard, hid themselves immediately. And Pietro, knowing that that warning must inevitably be discovered to be false, and that he himself would be condemned as a traitor, understood only too well the penalty which would be exacted later on. And you, as he also knew, would have been seen with him, and, as a supposed accomplice, be tracked home."

"But what league or society exists which finds it necessary to maintain such an extraordinary and elaborate system of spying?" cried Barry.

"Your question was answered from the moment when I heard of the letters scrawled upon the dead man's face, and saw the card which you received. Both Tutelli and Pietro were members or agents of one of the most powerful of international organizations, the Society of the Black Hand, or 'Mano Nera,' which, from its birthplace in Italy, has spread, with amazing rapidity and most devastating results, throughout the world. The society is especially powerful in the United States, and I learned recently that it has gained a foothold in England. No doubt the house in Latymer Grove was one of its headquarters. Pietro's profession was simply that of sentinel, even as those of the society are blackmail, robbery, and callous murder of the individual who may be unfortunate to stand in its path. In your own case it is clear that Tutelli, from a cranny in his place of concealment, or from the roof above, had seen your meeting with Pietro and the house you eventually entered (the door below would be perfectly visible in spite of the gloomy weather), and had afterwards gone down to meet the expostulating and explaining Pietro himself."

"And then?"

"Clearly one rogue failed to convince the other, and duly paid the penalty of nonsuccess. Indeed, I fancy that Tutelli must have realised that the warning was false before the other entered the house, for he had climbed up to reach down his instrument of vengeance—one of the eighteenth century duelling swords which hang in the hall."

"How did you arrive at that?" asked Coutts.

"The sword had been driven through the dead man's coat and braces, and had duly registered its peculiar four-sided shape upon them. Furthermore, there were microscopical traces of dust and rust upon the edges of the material. No doubt the fact that the sword was very rusty, and one which would conceal any traces of blood which might remain upon it, influenced Tutelli in his choice of a weapon. He put it back again, but he could not restore to it the dust which still lay thickly upon its fellow.

"I had as yet no clues as to the direction in which the murderer had fled, and the man had the advantage of a start of at least a day and half. But in one of the upper rooms I found a luggage-label— newly written, yet flung aside—which was in itself a perfect mine of information. It told me at once that the villains contemplated travelling far enough to make baggage necessary. The writing itself was in the hand of a woman—clearly a foreigner —and, by the vigorous formation of the characters, fairly young. It was the same as that on the card of Barry's, so that the two—man and woman—were concerned in and the murder and had fled together. Finally, the label had been addressed to a Sicillian port and then discarded, it was evident that they had changed their plans at the last moment for some vital reason.

"A glance at a shipping-list in the house told me why. They had just missed the boat, and from the same source I discovered their most likely alternative. A steamer was timed to leave Southampton for the States early to-morrow morning, and it was the earliest vessel in which they could escape the country.

"I made inquiries at the terminus, and at last I found a porter who remembered conveying the luggage of a hooky-nosed Italian gentleman, who walked slightly lame, and who was accompanied by a young, handsome woman of apparently the same nationally, on the Southampton express. On the strength of this information, I hurried to Scotland Yard, and succeeded in persuading our friend here to send a telegram to the police at the docks."

"There is one other point," said Barry, after an impressive little pause. "What became of the man who brought me the information concerning your 'accident'?"

"Well, knowing something of the gentleman with whom I was dealing, it was fairly obvious that an additional member of the gang would be deputed to keep an eye upon your movements. You would have been seen to call here, and although I have had no previous official dealings with the Society of the Black Hand, they would know me well enough to guess the reason of the visit. I was fairly confident that I should be shadowed, and also that they would do their best to get rid of the man who, by this time, would certainly be regarded as an arch-traitor."

"Well?" said Barry and Coutts together.

"I've no doubt our friend overheard my directions to the cabman, waited a little time, and then tried to lure you out. Failing in that, he hung about until I returned, as he knew I should, and then proceeded to follow me on foot to No. 11. There he was compelled to wait outside while I entered the house with a constable. The latter at length emerged, but I did not—at any rate, by the orthodox way—with the result that, as Carroll has since reported, the Italian unwisely attempted to enter the house in order to settle his doubts as to my whereabouts, and was promptly arrested."

"There may be danger in future," said Coutts.

"I think not. For, consider—Pietro is dead. Tutelli and the woman will soon, I hope, be placed beyond the power of inflicting vengeance, and the fourth member of the society has never come face to face with either Barry or myself. And—"

There was a sharp rap at the door.

"Telegram forwarded from Scotland Yard for you, sir," said Mrs. Bardell.

Coutts opened it and spread the crumpled sheet of paper upon the table.

"Tutelli and wife arrested at docks tonight," it ran. "Papers in their possession fully justify action."

The signature that followed was that of the inspector in charge at Southampton.

Blake drew a deep breath of relief.

"It's been an odd way of employing Sunday evening," he said, "but since we have laid a couple of the biggest villains in existence by the heels, I do not consider it ill-spent."

Our Magazine Corner.

IT is a curious fact that not only will men, and women, too, run almost any risk—even that of the hangman's rope—for the sake of possessing themselves of precious stones, but will sometimes spend small fortunes in the effort.

Attempts to steal such famous stones as the Hope Diamond are too well known to need describing here, but of other and equally interesting cases history is full.

There was the case of Colonel Blood's futile attempt to steal the Crown jewels from the Tower of London, and futile also was the effort to steal the Russian Crown jewels during the reign of the First Nicholas. Then followed the recent assassination of the late Czar and Czarina and the subsequent theft of jewels worth, perhaps, two million pounds.

One of the best-remembered robberies of recent years is probably that of a matchless pearl necklace in transit between Paris and London, in 1913. The execution of the theft cost some £3,000, as well as an amount almost as large which the robbers had to pay for their defence some months later—and all for no purpose.

This necklace, which was rightly described as the most wonderful in the world, was composed of perfectly matched rose pearls. Some idea of its value may be gained from the fact that it was insured for a sum of no less than £130,000. to gain possession of it a number of men plotted for months, finally serving long terms of imprisonment. And the irony of it all was that, after all the trouble they had gone to to obtain it, they had to abandon it by getting a confederate to "lose" it in the street, enclosed in a matchbox, in order to reduce the terms of imprisonment they knew was awaiting them, which would have been longer had the spoils been found on them.

Opportunity, of course, is the essence of theft, and for this reason the great railway termini have always proved a happy hunting ground for the expert jewel thief. In fact, most of the more noticeable and daring crimes of this description have been committed at these places.

No doubt the hurry and bustle connected with the departure or arrival of a well loaded train to or from the Continent or from the north, at the close of the shooting season, affords full opportunity for the man there for this purpose.

Take, for instance, the theft of the Duchess of Sutherland's jewel-case, with gems worth £25,000, from the Gare du Nord in Paris. The case had been placed on a rack in a first-class carriage by a maid, and while her back was turned someone stole the case and disappeared.

No trace of the thief or thieves was ever found, though there was no doubt in the minds of the police that the case had been stolen by one of the best-known expedients of jewel thieves, that of the "covering bag," a bottomless bag fitted with springs inside enabling anything it was placed over to be gripped and carried away, this method affording no opportunity for the case or bag to be recognised before the thief got clear away.

There was also the theft of the Countess Cowley's jewels from St. Pancras Station, and the Countess of Dudley's at Paddington, in both of which cases the loss was over £15,000.

It is more than likely that most of these gems adorn the fair neck of some Society beauty to-day having been re-cut and re-set so that their identification is a matter of impossibility.

By a strange coincidence, a few months after the theft of the Countess of Dudley's jewels, Baron Bulow, while going to visit her, was robbed at the same station of gems worth £15,000.

Hotels, too, have provided a happy hunting ground for the jewel thief. There was the robbery from the Marquis of Anglesea while staying at a Piccadilly hotel, for which a valet known to the fraternity as "Harry the Valet" was held responsible. There are, of course many others.

Daring—and luck—helped thieves to get away with diamonds worth £15,000 from the Hatton Garden Post Office, and again a parcel worth £20,000 from St. Martin's-le-Grand, besides another from the post-office in Southampton-Row some years later.

Mystery still surrounds the theft of a consignment of over £100,000 worth of pearls, diamonds, and sapphires sent to the Queen of Siam by steamer. Only two of these ever came to light, and they were found in possession of a man arrested in France. In this case the jewels were packed in a sealed box and placed in the strong-room of the steamer, the box being found empty on arrival, though the seals on it were intact.

www.ingramcontent.com/pod-product-compliance
Lightning Source LLC
Chambersburg PA
CBHW050824180626
46814CB00004B/1452